CASSIE & IKE

CASSIE & IKE

~ BY ~
Mary Carr Hanna

JOHN F. BLAIR, Publisher
Winston-Salem, North Carolina

c, 1

Copyright © 1973 by JOHN F. BLAIR, *Publisher*
Library of Congress Catalog Card Number: 73–77900
All rights reserved

ISBN 0–910244–70–7

Printed in the United States of America
by Heritage Printers, Inc.
Charlotte, North Carolina

NOV 2 '73   —BL

For Julie Hanna & Nicole Hanna

*whose great-great-grandmother's
letters provided the inspiration
for this book*

‿〈 I 〉‿

THIS MORNING, AS CASSIE BALLINGER SAT BESIDE HER MOTHER ON
the rough bench, her hands in their lace mitts folded demurely,
she had no wish to speak out in meeting and disagree with the
things that Friend Eunice Cox was saying. It was too fine a day
outside the high narrow windows. Autumn was such a good
time to be alive. The birds were singing in the forest beyond the
fence that enclosed the cemetery, and the soft sound of a cow-
bell came to her from far off in the woods, now beginning to
turn red and yellow.

Cassie had been tempted to pick some of the goldenrod growing along the fields, to pin it in the fold of her shawl as they
walked through the churchyard from the upping block where
she had dismounted, but she had resisted the temptation. There
were Friends in the meeting who would feel called upon to
frown at such vanity, although Cassie herself felt there was no
vanity in wishing to enjoy the beauty God sent, the gold of the
flowers against the grey of the shawl. She pushed back a curly
red tendril of hair that seemed set upon creeping forth and
testifying to a lack of plainness Cassie could not help if she
would.

Cassie thought fondly of her parents and felt a great thankfulness for the two of them, a thankfulness that became a kind
of prayer. Paul said Christians should pray without ceasing, but
Cassie knew few who did—only her mother, whose prayer was
one of serene joyfulness. Mother seemed always to shine with
that Inner Light about which George Fox had written.

Father was different. He was sometimes led by the spirit, but
not so constantly as Mother.

Father was on the other side of the partition separating the
men of the meeting from the women, and Cassie could not see
him. During the meeting for worship, the shutters in the parti-

I

tion had been open; now that the business session had begun, they were closed. But as she thought of her father, there among the men, the face of the young man newly come to the community and the meeting returned to her. It was with difficulty that she restrained the smile that seemed to come unbidden to her lips. This was no time for such thoughts.

Cassie looked with love at her mother's hands, hardened by the toil of a pioneer household, and then, with a little shame, she looked at her own, so white against the grey of her dress. Truly it was no fault of hers that her mother—and especially her father—felt that she was better employed learning to read and to write, studying the books and magazines that came to them from the East, than learning the household tasks so unfailingly taught to the daughters of Friends. Indeed, it had only been in the last few years that Mother had allowed her to learn to cook and sew, to take the time from her studies and, more particularly, to deprive Father of the pleasure it gave him to teach her the things he knew. In no other house in the meeting was there such great respect for knowledge.

Cassie had not gone to the seminary as she would have liked, primarily because her father would not part with her companionship; instead, he had taught her from his own great store of knowledge. Father had come to Indiana originally from the East, and he had attended an eastern college. Often he made trips to his old home and attended Yearly Meeting there, frequently returning with some new poem written by his friend, John Greenleaf Whittier.

Cassie privately thought that Father himself could write poems if he would, but Father laughed at her and told her she was prejudiced, that it would be through Cassie herself that he would be remembered. But he encouraged her to write poems and once would have sent one of them to Whittier to read, had his daughter been willing.

2

Although the Friends were noted for their respect for schooling, the Ballinger family knew that many in the meeting disapproved of the learning Cassie received from her father. Thus, it had come as no surprise when the Oversight and Ministry Committee rode up to the Ballinger home one winter evening.

Father greeted them calmly. "Samuel Evans, Wesley Evans, won't you have chairs?" The flush in his cheeks spoke of displeasure.

Mother's expression was anxious. She found contention in the meeting painful, and Father sometimes enjoyed an opportunity to expose what he considered the pretensions of some of the more outwardly pious Friends.

Cassie thought of the Evans brothers now on the men's side of the partition and remembered how uncomfortable they had seemed during their call on Father, how loath they had been to explain the purpose of their call.

After some remarks about the weather, the plentiful harvest now in, and the health of the members of the meeting, the visitors had sat silent and reluctant to continue until Father said, his tone almost a question, "You are kind to call on such a cold evening. You are most welcome."

Samuel Evans began. "William Ballinger, we have come to talk with thee as to the schooling thee is giving thy daughter."

"You have?"

Wesley Evans now spoke. "Some of the meeting do not feel thee is wise in the kind of learning thee is giving her. Thee is not preparing her to be a good and helpful wife in this land where women must be able to do things not required in the East where thee was reared."

Cassie saw the flush heighten on Father's cheek and sensed Mother's anxiety. Mother's love and loyalty to Father were so great that she would never interfere at such a time. But Cassie admitted to herself that there was truth in what the committee was saying.

"Thee has not encouraged thy daughter to help thy wife, as other young women in the community do," Samuel Evans continued.

Father was on his feet. "Has thee heard complaints from my wife? Does thee feel free to speak for my wife? Does she seem overworked to thee, unhappy in her lot?"

"William, William," Mother said gently, "they do not come to speak of thy treatment of thy wife. Thee knows I have no complaint of thee or of Cassie."

Father cooled a little, but Samuel Evans was cautious. "It does not seem fitting that a young woman should spend her time in learning Greek and Latin when there are more useful pursuits for her."

"Thee may make thy report to the meeting," Father replied firmly, "that Cassie Ballinger does not spend her time in light or mischievous behavior, that her mother is well able to judge what skills she will need. And if Cassie should choose to marry any young Friend in the meeting, she will be able to do the things needful in a godly home."

Then Mother had been moved to pray, after which the Oversight and Ministry Committee had left with unusual speed, as though they regretted having come in the first place.

After the committee had left, Father was thoughtful, and it was some little time before he muttered, "Meddlesome. Interfering."

Mother replied softly, her voice concerned. "William, William, thee must not be harsh with them. Thee knows they have not had thy schooling. They do not understand thy feeling."

Unmoved by the committee's protest, Father had continued his teaching. Cassie, however, wondered, not unlike the ladies

4

in the meeting, to what use she could put her learning. She would indeed teach the school when fall came, but there were few who would wish to learn the Latin and Greek she knew.

Father could read the Bible in Greek and Hebrew, and sometimes he said it did not always mean the same to him in the English translation. No doubt there would be value in reading the Word of God thus, but, on the other hand, it was Father's belief that God would show a man what was right and what was wrong, that God's spirit was more final than the Scriptures, whether one read them in Greek or in English.

Now Cassie listened to Friend Eunice Cox's voice: "A committee should be appointed to look into the gatherings held at the homes of our young people. Too many are welcomed who are not of our faith. You must all see it can lead only to trouble and marrying out of the meeting." Eunice Cox's voice was slightly more complaining this morning than usual.

Cassie tried to close her mind to the words and felt her mother's hand press lightly on her own. Was it so plain, then, that her thoughts were not here in this meeting, but in some far place woolgathering? Cassie returned the pressure and saw the relief in her mother's glance.

Often Cassie had wondered if she was to be a trial to Mother. Poor Mother, always caught between her wish for harmony in her family and her desire for peace with the meeting, which was so often not in agreement with her forward-thinking husband. At times Cassie had thought that Mother would have preferred it if she were more like the other young women in the meeting, but knew that her daughter's likeness to Father Ballinger was too great for this to be. More often Cassie believed that, in reality, Mother would not want her to be like the others; she loved Father too much and was too much one with him in most things to wish to have her daughter different.

Cassie was aware that Father hoped she might find some

5

young man from the East, as learned as himself, who would come for some purpose to this new settlement and appreciate the paragon of learning and virtue Father believed he had been instrumental in fashioning. At times, Cassie also believed that this might happen. But at other times, she found it more likely that she would be a spinster, spending her life teaching the children of others.

Mother sometimes feared that Father had made Cassie so different with his educating and book-learning that she would be unhappy as the wife of a pioneer farmer and that, if she did not wish to be an old maid, it would be well for her to take a greater part in the life of the young people of the community. Mother had said, "It is not good to be stand-offish if thee wishes to be happy in thy life."

Well, Cassie would see. Mayhap schoolteaching would bring some great adventure to her, though it seemed most unlikely that adventure could come from the little country schoolhouse, which the Friends had built so proudly as soon as the meeting house was finished.

Cassie felt a queer warmth and excitement not caused by the sun outside or by the sound of Eunice Cox's voice as she told of her revelation as she had washed up the dishes on Third Day last week.

What was it about this morning that made it seem different from the usual First Day morning? Surely it could not be the new young man, here for the second time, on the other side of the partition. Seventeen was not so old that she should begin to dream dreams about a young man of such a solemn, almost lugubrious, countenance!

Cassie well knew, however, that there was not another young woman of her age in the meeting who was not aware of this young man. Although the Ballingers were old settlers in the community, having come here in the 1820's long before Cassie was born, new people came to this land from other meetings every few months. If there were young, unmarried men among them, there was great excitement on the benches where the marriageable girls were seated.

Cassie controlled a smile. It had been a strange thing that had happened last First Day as the general meeting was about to begin. Cassie, her eyes cast down, had been sitting modestly in her seat, very close to the partition. She had heard a shuffling of feet on the other side of the partition and had turned her head to see what brother walked so heavily. With a slight sense of shock, she had looked at the feet that were now in her line of vision.

They were little different from the feet she saw there every First Day morning—except in size. Indeed, she thought in wonder, she had never seen such feet. Truly it was a strange thing to look at a man's feet and only his feet. It must be an unprepossessing young man to have such a large understanding.

It seemed a little unfair to judge a man by his feet alone, especially when they were so oversized. Clearly they did not belong to any of the brothers who usually came to the meeting.

As Cassie raised her eyes gradually, an astonishing length of limb began to be revealed, a length of limb not adequately covered by the pants upon it. It was as though this person, having reached his full growth, had not been able to replace his outgrown trousers.

Now, in spite of herself, Cassie's gaze followed the limb, and suddenly she was looking directly into a pair of dark blue, long-lashed eyes set deep in the weathered face of a young man. Something about this man's face and figure indicated clearly that he was one who made his living by tilling the earth, as did most of the men here.

He was a strange young man, not long in the community. Cassie would not have forgotten him had she seen him before.

7

Suddenly, something about the solemnity of his face above such enormous feet and lengthy limbs, so scantily covered, struck Cassie as funny. Father was of Huguenot ancestry, and she must have inherited from him a Gallic sense of humor. But she must not allow herself to laugh *at* anyone, particularly at such a time and place. But in spite of her resolve, Cassie felt the corners of her mouth lift in amusement.

At once she knew, from the young man's expression, that he had seen her smile and did not condone this merriment in the meeting house, possibly at his expense. His long upper lip pressed firmly against his lower one in disapproval, and Cassie was hard put to restrain the wider smile she felt creeping up on her. Young men did not usually frown when Cassie smiled at them, though she was not given to flirtation. What manner of man was this?

Perhaps he was married and his wife was here among the women, watching the frown on her husband's face and wondering what unmaidenly young woman had brought such displeasure to him. Cassie looked quickly across the little meeting house and saw no other stranger there.

Then she was struck by a resemblance. Of course! This young man looked like the Evans brothers, neighbors of the Ballingers, who had come here with the first settlers.

Cassie remembered having heard that their younger brother had purchased a farm across from the schoolhouse where Cassie was to teach. It had been a matter of scant importance, for she had felt that anyone even remotely related to the Evanses could be of no interest to her.

It must indeed be this young man who had already looked at Cassie and found her forward, perhaps unmaidenly.

Cassie dropped her eyes in confusion, a little indignant that she should mind if this young man did not approve of her glance. Yet she herself would not like her first look from a young

8

man to be one of amusement because of some feature which she could in no way help. She should be ashamed, and indeed she would be ashamed, when the service was over and she had time to think about it.

But Cassie was unable to resist another glance at the solemn newcomer.

Now, a week later, as she waited for the women's business meeting to be over, she thought with scorn that she could never be interested in any man so solemn. The man who could interest Cassie must have a humor like Father's, not a near frown on his face, and that because a young woman had looked at him with a smile.

She remembered little of what had been said in the meeting for worship this morning. The silence had fitted well with Cassie's mood, though she had found it harder than usual to bring her mind to thoughts of God.

Or were thoughts of the beauty of the autumn morning and the life before her pleasing to God? Truly Cassie had only wishes for a good and righteous life. Firmly she said a little prayer that her thoughts, too, might be righteous and pleasing to God.

At last the meeting was over, and they filed from the church. As she and Mother waited for Father to bring the horses, Wesley Evans paused with his brother beside him and said politely, "Faith Ballinger, this is our young brother Ike, come from southern Indiana to live in our neighborhood and be part of our meeting. Ike, this is Cassie Ballinger, who will teach the school across from thy house this fall."

Cassie curtsied gravely and felt the warm blood rise in her cheeks. What could be wrong with her that she should be troubled by a meeting with a young man, a brother of the Evans family, who held themselves to be very righteous, although the

9

Ballingers did not agree with this estimate at times? Father had even been heard to mutter, in the bosom of his family, the word "self-righteous" when their righteousness was mentioned, which was most unlike Father, who did not often speak harshly of others.

To be sure, it had been Wesley and Samuel Evans who had called on Father to speak as to the wisdom of his upbringing of his only daughter. No doubt they had already warned Ike of the unseemliness of Cassie's rearing, of her lack of womanly skills. It would doubtless be most unpleasing to them if this brother should find Cassie comely in spite of their advice in the matter.

Again Cassie felt that unbidden smile come to her lips. She must be more careful, or this young man would believe that she was of a flirtatious disposition—and nothing could be more untrue, as anyone in the meeting could tell him.

ON NEXT FIRST DAY CASSIE SAT FAR FROM THE PARTITION, DETERmined that no one should know that for the last fortnight her mind had dwelt too often on the newcomer from southern Indiana. She kept her eyes firmly to the front or on her folded hands.

Only after everyone was seated did she allow her glance to move quickly over the men on the rough benches. Her heart sank in disappointment when she saw that the youngest Evans brother was not there. The thought came that, perhaps, he had returned to his home in the south and would not be back to take over his farm.

Throughout the following week, Cassie listened for news of Ike Evans when Father returned from the store or from a visit to the neighbors. But neither of her parents seemed even aware of Ike Evans's existence, and she would not ask about him.

Cassie had been very busy with her final preparations for the teaching of the school. It would soon be time for lessons to begin, and she wished to be firmly grounded in the things she would teach.

When the last teacher had married, there had been no one who wished or was able to take the school. Many of the parents had come to her or to her father and asked that she teach for at least a year. The school would be quite large this year, and since it was a subscription school, Father felt that this was a kind of reward for Cassie's upbringing and education.

Still, Cassie had some misgivings as to her fitness for the task she was about to undertake. It was not that she doubted her knowledge, for Father's teaching had been thorough. But she sometimes feared her ability to discipline the older boys and girls. The enrollment was larger this year than last, and then the teacher had had trouble with discipline. Cassie trusted that the parents' faith in her would not be misplaced.

Many of the students were older than Cassie herself. Would she be able to enforce the rules she would have to lay down? Or would the pupils laugh at her and refuse to do as she bade? Plainly she could not use the rod on a boy twice her size.

Among the pupils would be the children of Wesley and Samuel Evans, some of them almost grown men. Perhaps Ike would come at recess or before school to send messages to his brothers, and in this way she might become acquainted with him.

At any rate, this strange preoccupation that she had with the youngest Evans brother had taken her mind from her worries about the school. Not that she did not still wish to do a good job, but she seemed unable to keep her mind upon it now. Father would begin to talk about her work, and she would have to bring her mind back from far away to answer him. This was most unusual, for Cassie found his words interesting and worthwhile as a rule. It was not mere respect for her parents, as the Scriptures commanded, but sincere admiration and love that produced the attention Cassie usually gave him.

On Sixth Day before Second Day when school was to open, Cassie woke with a kind of bubbling excitement. This was the day that Father would drive her to the schoolhouse to take her supplies and to be sure that all was ready for the arrival of the children and their teacher.

All the past week, Cassie had wished to ask Father to take her to the schoolhouse. She had refused to give in to her impulse, since it was actually a desire to see the house where Ike Evans was making his home—and a hope that she might catch a glimpse of him and try again to learn what there was about his awkward figure that took her mind from all the things which, before, had seemed important.

Father was lending her his *Encyclopedia Americana* in case there should be need for it. Cassie had hesitated to accept his offer, knowing how much he prized the books with their leather binding and their gold-edged leaves, but nothing would do but that she take them with her. There was small chance that the rowdier students would look in them and soil them. Their *McGuffey's Readers* and the copy of the Holy Scriptures prescribed in the discipline of the meeting would be enough to occupy the time these pupils would wish to spend in learning.

Father was, as usual, willing and able to give Cassie much good advice on how to handle the young people. Once, when another teacher could not be found, Father himself had taught the school, not wishing to leave the young people untaught.

Now he said to his daughter, "Thee must be sure, Cassie, that thy pupils have no question as to thy confidence in thyself and thy knowledge. Yet it would be most unwise for thee to pretend to knowledge thee does not have. Then they will not attempt to heckle or confuse thee."

"Yes, Father, I will remember, but thee knows it will be hard to impress the Jones or Nicholson boys with my age and size. They are all older and weigh near twice as much."

"Size and weight are no measure of authority, Cassie. Thee well knows that to be true."

"Yes, Father, thee is no giant thyself, but everyone in the community well knows thee is to be respected."

"Thee means thee does not think thy father a big man? Thee is pretty small thyself to speak with disrespect of the size of anyone else. Thee had better speak with more respect, or thee may receive the chastisement thee was spared as a child!" Father's smile was mischievous, for he liked for Cassie to tease him, to make him feel that they were comrades, not merely father and daughter.

Cassie's words were earnest. "Father, thee has shown me all my life that it is not necessary to use force to command respect and obedience. Else I would not feel capable of teaching this school."

"Thee is right, but thee will find that some of these boys and girls are more accustomed to the switch than to the reason thy mother and I have used with thee. It may be hard. But with God's help, thee will win through. I do not fear for thee."

The sun was bright as Cassie and her father traveled down the narrow road in the light spring wagon, and a crisp chill in the air made Cassie's cheeks red and cold. But as they came in sight of the schoolhouse and, across from it, the house where Ike

Evans now lived, Cassie felt a sudden warmth in her cheeks, and she was sure there was a redness there not caused by the cold air or the chill of the wind.

A thin line of smoke rose from the chimney of the weather-beaten little house still surrounded by the summer's grass. It was clear that much cleaning had been done around the place, but it was chiefly around the barn, as befitted a man's interest. Surely his sisters-in-law, Rachel and Priscilla, would clean the house and make it cheerful for him, Cassie thought. She felt a great wave of sympathy for so solemn a young man, alone with no one to care for him or to cheer him.

Her cheeks felt as if they were burning with a fever. She stole a quick look at Father and was relieved that he seemed unconscious of her inspection of the little farm across the way.

Now Father's voice was serious, grave. "Cassie, does thee think thee is ready for this new undertaking? Thee knows that unless thee really wishes to do this, thee need not. Thy father can care for thee without thy earning thy living."

Cassie made her voice firm in spite of her misgivings and of her strange interest in the farm across the way. "Father, thee knows that I wish to teach this school. Thee can see that it is time thy daughter did something to show that the learning thee has given her is not wasted. Thy neighbors already believe that thee has not fitted me for housewifely duties. Thee would not wish for thy daughter to be entirely worthless."

Father Ballinger laid his hand on his daughter's cheek and said fondly, "Cassie, Cassie, thee should not say these things, even in jest. Thee will have thy old father saying, like the Evanses, 'Idle words, idle words!' " With the mention of the name, his glance fell on the little house across the way.

Cassie felt a quick fear that Father would be reminded of the things he did not like about this young man's family and, in so doing, would place Ike in a category with his brothers.

But his voice held only neighborly interest as he said, "That reminds me, Cassie, did thee know that the young brother of the Evanses has taken the farm across the way, is to live there alone and farm it?"

He continued kindly. "He comes from southern Indiana, seems like a good young man, a little lacking in humor, but of a kinder turn than his brothers Wesley and Samuel, I believe. I saw him in the store." Then with a humorous twinkle, "No doubt there will soon be a young lady who will be glad to share the place with him, to provide him with the wife every young farmer needs."

Cassie answered slowly, careful that none of the interest she did not like or understand should show in her voice. "Thee is probably right, Father. His brother Wesley presented him to Mother and to me two weeks ago on First Day."

Was there a sharpness in Father's glance? Had she been unable to hide her interest? Cassie felt herself flush again.

"Did thee think him a likely young man, daughter?"

"He seemed like a sober young man, almost a mournful young man. With an astonishing length of foot and limb." She shuddered delicately, and Father smiled—deceived, she hoped, concerning her interest.

Why did she feel ashamed and disloyal, as she would have felt had she said something unkind about Father or Mother? It was not because she had tried to deceive Father. She must do that for his peace of mind, for Father would be most unhappy should she be interested as yet in any young man, particularly—

When they arrived at the school, Cassie looked quickly over the room and saw that all was as she wished. The women of the community had scrubbed the place well, and the parents had furnished a great supply of wood, which was carefully corded outside the back door.

While Father was unloading the wagon, Cassie stood by, but

she was unable to prevent her eyes from straying to Ike Evans's farmhouse. As she watched discreetly, the side door opened. The tall young man who seemed never to have left her thoughts came out with a dishpan of water in his hands, stepped far away from the house—like a man who had been taught that he must not do things that would draw flies to the kitchen door—and threw the dishwater over the rail fence that separated the barnyard from the dooryard. Taking the dishcloth which he held, he wiped out the pan, then hung it on a nail by the door.

Again Cassie felt that unreasonable sympathy for this young man who had to do the farm work around the place and, at the same time, was forced to do his own cooking and housework. Surely he was a young man in need of a wife, desperate need.

She considered the marriageable young women of the community and was struck with the thought that none among them seemed quite suitable. Her mind passed over the young women of her acquaintance, the ones in the meeting, for of course no young Friend would wish to marry out of the meeting. Not that this had never happened, but it was a thought one would not entertain until one was forced to. Even Cassie herself, who was, she must admit, of a rebellious nature at times, had never considered with real seriousness that she could marry any man not of her faith, no matter how admirable he might be in other ways. That would be unthinkable.

To be sure, there was Sara Newby, a young woman who could take this little house and make it neat and shining, a fit place for a young farmer with his way to make in the world. Sara was skilled with a needle, could weave if that were necessary—though little of that kind of work was done here now. She could make the finest of soap, and her butter and cheese were the admiration of the women in the meeting. She had a chest filled with quilts, which she had made herself. The stitches were of incredible smallness. She could also tailor a man's suit, would no doubt be able to make pants more appropriate in length for the long limbs of Ike Evans. His shirts would be well made, too, from the brown jean cloth and would never lack for buttons. Cassie smothered a sigh.

For almost the first time, she was sorry that her skill in this kind of work was so limited. Somehow, she had believed with Father that there would be little use for her to learn such skills, though Mother had often felt that she should have been taught more of these things. Before, she had never honestly regretted it. Now she wondered a little.

Then Cassie thought, somewhat comforted, that Sara Newby was not a young woman who would bring a warming smile to the face of this young man. And it might well be that making him smile would be a greater blessing than being able to take good care of his house and clothing.

Now, as if from a long way off, Cassie heard Father speaking, a little loudly for him. "Cassie, did thee not hear me speak to thee? Thee is indeed woolgathering today. Is it the thought of the teaching of thy school? Or—"

Cassie interrupted quickly. "Excuse me, Father. I am still a little concerned with the thought of disciplining the older boys and girls. Does thee truly think me fitted for that discipline?"

Father's tone was reassuring. "Thee will get on well, never fear, daughter. Thee has dignity, and that will serve thee well in this case."

"Thank thee, Father. Thee will help me with thy faith."

Her words were as they should be, but inwardly Cassie had a feeling of deceit. Usually there was great clearness between her and Father.

When they drove away, Cassie was careful that her glance did not wander back to the little house with its grey loneliness.

⌐ III ⌐

THE GREATEST PORTION OF THE FALL FARM WORK HAD TO BE well out of the way before the older children could leave for school, so it was beginning to be quite chilly the morning that classes began. Cassie left home early in the little spring wagon in order to build the fire and have the schoolhouse warm. She wanted no excuse for the excessive movement of hands and feet because of the chill.

An hour before the pupils were to come, Cassie reached the school. As she approached the grounds, she saw the white smoke rising from the farmhouse across the way. She tied her horse to the fence and began to unhitch him from the light wagon.

Suddenly Cassie heard a noise behind the schoolhouse. Quickly she lowered the shafts and backed the wagon away from the horse's heels. Then she hurried around to the back of the building.

As she approached, the noise became louder. Could it be that already some of the older pupils were bent on trouble for the new teacher? There were cases in this new country where teachers had been locked from their schoolrooms.

But this was even worse than that. The great rick of wood, furnished for the school year and carefully corded outside the back door, now lay in a great pile blocking the entrance. Beyond it, a cow—enormous in Cassie's eyes, for milking was another housewifely art in which she was not grounded—stood calmly chewing her cud, but eying Cassie in a manner that appeared most unfriendly. Cassie stared in fright and indignation. Though she was well skilled in riding and did not fear a horse, there was something frightening about the long horns of this creature.

And somewhere under the great pile of wood was the kindling she would need for building her fire.

"Shoo! Get out of here, thee brute!"

The cow would not shoo. She seemed quite at home and not belligerent until Cassie moved toward her. Then she lowered her head menacingly and lifted a hoof as though about to attack.

Cassie stood helplessly. Finally she picked up a stick of wood and told herself she must somehow force this creature to return to wherever she belonged. No cow would disrupt her school.

Then a thought struck her. Of course, this brute must belong to Ike Evans. There was no other house nearby. Well, she would go and tell that young man that his creature had done great damage to her woodpile.

Looking warily behind her in case the cow should decide to attack her from the rear, Cassie hurried across the road and knocked at the front door, feeling a sense of excitement and anticipation that had nothing to do with the cow behind the schoolhouse.

No one answered, and Cassie rushed around to the side door. As she stepped up onto the stoop, she could see through the window that the young man was about to sit down to his breakfast. No doubt, she told herself with an attempt at indignation, he had milked his cow and then turned her loose to wander, with never a thought of the damage she might do to young women bent on doing their duty to their pupils! She would certainly remonstrate with him about such unneighborly conduct. She knocked on the door.

He stared through the window at her in such a manner that Cassie would have said he looked entirely daft, had it been any other young man. He shook his head as if to clear it, as if this must be a dream. Cassie knocked again, quite loudly this time.

He rose hastily, and so quick was he in his movement that the chair fell over with a little crash, and he made no move to right it. Two long steps brought him to the door. He opened it quickly.

"Cassie Ballinger! Thee is here? How did thee get here?"

Ah, so he knew her name, remembered it from that one meeting. No doubt he had heard about her faults from his brothers and sisters-in-law.

Cassie made her voice stern, indignant. "Thy cow! Does thee know perchance where thy cow is this morning?"

"My cow?"

He sounded as though he had never heard of a cow. Surely a stupid young man. Or one who was still a little dazed by the surprise of her visit.

"Yes, thy cow! Thee knows what a cow is."

What was the matter with her that she should be so rude to a strange young man? Particularly a young man with so solemn an expression, one who might well be easily offended and who had perhaps already been offended by the smile she had been unable to restrain on that First Day?

Cassie continued, quite determined to erase the hurt look from his face. Her voice was gentle, almost loving, as befitted Christian brethren. "Thy cow must have strayed from thy barn. She is in the schoolyard. Will thee come with me and bring her home?" Cassie did not even mention the damage to the woodpile.

He followed Cassie obediently, his face red through the summer's brown. As they rounded the corner of the schoolhouse and he saw the havoc the cow had wrought, he struck the animal smartly on her flank.

"Thee troublesome brute! Get home!"

The cow ambled slowly away. Ike stood in confusion before Cassie; his hands, reddened by the fall winds and the washing of the dishes, hung awkwardly at his sides.

"I am sorry, Cassie Ballinger. I will cord thy wood again."

"Thee need not trouble thyself, Ike Evans. But I would build a fire before school opens, if thee will find me some kindling. Mine is under the wood."

His voice was eager. "I will build thy fire. I will bring some kindling from my own pile. Do not distress thyself."

In spite of his height and apparent awkwardness, he moved with ease and dispatch when there was a use for his hands. Soon a good fire was roaring up the chimney from the iron stove.

Looking at her hands, he said gently, "Thee should not carry these pieces of wood anyway. This is a man's work."

Cassie thought a little ruefully that Ike would not be wise to find himself a wife whose hands were too delicate to carry a few sticks of wood, if he were to have the kind of helpmeet he needed in the little house across the way.

But she answered him politely. "The big boys will carry some in for the morrow. Father would have come had he been at home, but he left this morning to go East for a few weeks."

"Thee may be sure I will come over this evening and put back the wood that the cow has knocked down. I will wait until the pupils have gone home so that I may not disturb thy school. Thee is not very big to have the ordering of a school," he added shyly. "But I can see thee is able."

"Thank thee, Ike Evans."

"If thee should need any assistance, thee has only to call, and I will come. There may be some troublesome lads in thy classes."

A good sense of security came to Cassie. "Thank thee. I can see that thee could indeed quiet any disturbance. But I trust all will go well, and I will not need to call upon thee."

"I believe thee will get on well with the young ones. Thee

has a way of dignity about thee." Then, as if surprised at his forwardness, he added, "I will return this evening. Farewell." He hurried away.

Cassie resisted a wish to stand and watch him until he got into the house. She hastened to her desk.

⤙ IV ⤚

Soon the children began to file into the building, some of them as shy as Cassie herself, some of them with a swagger that might bode ill for her if she allowed it to disconcert her.

For a moment Cassie thought that she might well have to call Ike Evans to help enforce her rules; then suddenly all her misgivings were gone. She felt an assurance that she would get on well with these boys and girls, would enjoy teaching them the things she had learned.

There being no bell, Cassie called clearly and loudly, "Books! Books!" As if by magic, there was stillness in the room, and she began the business of seating the pupils on the rough benches. The autumn sun shone in through the windows and seemed to make the whole room warm and friendly.

At recess and noon, the children offered to pile the wood up again, but Cassie told them they should enjoy the rest from school and not take that time for working. She organized games to take them away from the wood, but still some of them insisted on beginning to stack it. She soon saw that the task would not be finished in a few hours. There would be plenty of work for Ike Evans to do that evening, and for several days.

As soon as the last student had gone, Cassie began to clean the room for the next day's classes. She heard a knock at the back door and hurried to open it. Ike stood there smiling gravely.

"I have come to work on the wood."

"Thee need not neglect thy own work at home. The children will work on it betimes."

His voice was stiff with dignity and pride. "I wish to repair the damage done by my animal."

Cassie smiled at him, and his face softened. There was a kind of gentleness about Ike Evans's eyes that stayed even when his mouth and lips were stern, as though he had a natural sweetness of disposition, perhaps even humor, that was held in check by his early training.

"Then I shall help thee for a while," Cassie replied.

"Thee might just watch and talk to me as I work."

"No, I will help."

Together they stacked the wood, Cassie unskillfully, but Ike with an easy movement that Cassie admired. She saw him shift the sticks that she had awkwardly laid not quite straight, and she felt no resentment at this apparent criticism of her work.

To her amazement Cassie realized that the sun was dropping very low in the west, though it seemed but minutes since they had begun their work. Her home was three miles from the school, and if she did not start, it would be dark before she arrived there. Mother would be alarmed should night fall and Cassie still be on the way. It had not been many years since Indians and wild animals had lurked in these woods, and Mother had not forgotten.

"I must go now or my mother will worry. Thee must not work any longer, either. It is not urgent."

"Will thee let me return tomorrow evening? Perhaps thee would keep me company as I work."

"That would be very pleasant, Ike Evans."

"Could thee mayhap call me Ike?"

23

Cassie knew that this would not be maidenly, that the sisters in the meeting would think her forward. If Wesley and Samuel Evans were to hear of it, they, too, would think her forward, not a fit companion for their brother. But even with all of these things in her mind Cassie could not, for the life of her, restrain the answer that came to her lips.

"I've been calling thee Ike to myself ever since I saw thee on that First Day." Though her eyes were downcast, her words sounded loud and bold to her.

Ike's voice held a tremor no one could mistake. "Thee has? Thee has? Oh, Cassie!"

Cassie knew then that no declaration Ike might make at some later time would tell her more of how he felt about her, that he had said it all in the way he had spoken her name.

Surely he, too, had had her in his thoughts. That must have been the reason for his words when he saw her on his steps this morning: "Cassie Ballinger! Thee is here? How did thee get here?" Could it be that he had been imagining her across his table, eating breakfast with him? Cassie felt the heat in her cheeks, the warmth that had so embarrassed her when she had come here with Father.

Ike spoke solemnly, portentously, with a dignity equal to that of his brothers at their most dignified. "Would thee be willing for me to ask thy father to allow me to call on thee?"

Then, boyishly, his solemnity lightened, as if he could not restrain his words. "Oh, Cassie! Thee must know I have been waiting for thee all my life, doesn't thee?"

Cassie forgot all the things she had required in a husband: the learning, the wealth perhaps, the things so different from what this tall and, she had once thought, shy young man had to offer. She only knew that this Ike was the one she could somehow comfort and make happy. Between them they could find happiness and perchance a little gaiety—enough to make life a very

24

special thing, not humdrum or hard, though they might live in poor circumstances.

Suddenly thoughtful of what others would say, Cassie replied, "Thee had best not tell thy brothers thy plans for coming to call on me. They will find thy choice not to their liking, I fear."

Ike looked at her in surprise. "Thee must be wrong, Cassie. They have told me that no more worthy young woman lives in this community than thee."

"They did not tell thee that my father is not always in favor with the meeting? They did not mention that?"

"They said thy father was a worthy man, a little forward-thinking sometimes, but a worthy man."

"Did thee ask them about me, Ike?"

"They told me many things of thee and thy parents without my asking. No doubt they could see that I wished to hear. Cassie, the Lord sent me to this place here by the schoolhouse to find thee. Does thee think that?"

Cassie had been taught that the Lord led his children in the right way if they were willing to listen and to hear his words. Now she knew that it was indeed true. What else could account for their knowledge that this was meant to be—a knowledge gained so quickly?

"Yes, Ike, it must have been the Lord who led me to the teaching of this school. And thy cow, Ike, does thee think *she* was led?"

From the surprise on Ike's face, Cassie saw that he would have to be guided slowly to the paths of gaiety, that he felt the bringing of a cow into his declaration of devotion was not fitting.

Quickly, to take his mind from her ill-timed levity, she added, "It would be a fortunate thing if the brothers and sisters in the meeting could feel that this was a leading of the Lord, if Father could be justified with them for his part in it. They find it hard to believe so much learning is good for a woman. Does thee mind, that I have some learning?"

Ike gazed at her with such admiration on his face that Cassie felt well paid for the hours she had spent in getting her learning, and for the criticism she had borne from the brothers and sisters in the meeting. If Ike felt so about it, surely it had been right and proper all the while, not just a whim of Father's and of hers. While many of the Friends were proud that Lucretia Mott was one of them, they were not so ready to grant her beliefs to the women of their own families. But Father believed firmly in the equality of women and lived his beliefs with his wife and daughter.

AS CASSIE DROVE INTO THE BARNYARD, SHE FELT AS THOUGH Mother would be able to tell, just by looking at her, that something had happened to make the whole world seem different. She handed the reins to Caleb White, the hand who lived in the little log cabin where Father and Mother had first lived, then went into the house and laid her books on the kitchen table.

Mother turned from the stove and looked at her. "I see thee had no trouble today. Does thee like teaching school?"

"Oh, yes, Mother. The children were very good, and everything went well."

That was indeed true. If only she could tell someone how well it had gone! But now she would keep it a secret just between herself and Ike, until it would seem reasonable for them to be so fond of each other. Mother would think this was very quick, though no doubt she, more than Father, would find Ike very satisfactory as a son.

"It seems very lonesome without thy father tonight. But he enjoys these trips to Philadelphia, and we must not hold him back for any selfish reason."

"Thee is right, Mother. It seems already that it has been a week since Father left, and it was only this morning."

Mother Ballinger smiled with understanding at Cassie. "Thee knows I have always been glad that thee should love thy father so much, even if it should be more than thee loved me. It is good for a daughter to have such a tender father. All fathers are not like that."

"Mother, thee knows I do not love Father more than thee; only in a different way."

"Thee is very like thy father." Mother's tone was a little concerned. "Thy father, sometimes, is too ready to form his own opinions. It will go hard with a wife who wishes to form her own opinions. Thy husband may well find this troublesome in thee."

"Oh, no, Mother, he will be patient with me, I am sure!"

Mother carefully laid down the big iron spoon with which she had been stirring the gravy and turned to her quickly.

"Why, Cassie, thee speaks as if thee were thinking of someone especially!"

Cassie felt the flush that had bothered her several times recently, more than in all her life before. She could not keep her secret long if she spoke in this way!

"Thee knows, Mother, that when girls are as old as I, they do think of the husband they may have someday."

"Yes, I know; most girls do. But I thought thee did not. Well, it is time thee thought of a husband. I want thee to have one as good as thy father. Not like thy father maybe, for two

27

like thy father together would be in hot water often, I fear. Thee had better get thee a man who is not so advanced as thy father."

Three weeks ago Cassie would have insisted that the man she wanted must be like Father. Already she knew that Ike was as different from Father as a good sturdy homespun shirt was from the white ones that Father would be wearing tonight in Philadelphia.

Perhaps one's tastes might change when one became acquainted with the good qualities of a sturdy work shirt. And maybe Mother was right that Cassie would need someone more practical than she. Maybe Father wouldn't have got on so well himself without Mother to hold him back a bit.

Cassie found it hard to settle down to preparing her assignments for the next day, and more than once it seemed that Mother was looking at her questioningly.

The next day went quickly, and before she realized it, the children were gone. Almost at once, she heard Ike at work behind the schoolhouse. She waited a few moments, straightening the room, so that he would not think her forward.

Cassie smiled. After all, he might well think that she had been forward enough already. Mother would surely not have approved the thing she had told him about thinking of him as Ike since first she had seen him. It was more the kind of thing that Father would say if it came to him to say it.

At last she opened the back door and looked at him almost shyly—Cassie had never thought herself shy. "Good evening, Ike Evans."

Ike dropped the piece of wood he had picked up and hurried to the door. The steps were steep and narrow, and Ike reached up to assist her.

Only last week Cassie had raced Father from the back lot, through the woods, even jumping a low rail fence, but it was nice to have Ike's rough palm around hers. As Cassie stood on the second step, she saw suddenly that this made her just the same height as Ike.

She stopped. "My, but thee is tall, Ike."

"Thee is not very tall, Cassie; that is it."

Cassie was not sure whether she swayed a little, though it could well have been. So many things Cassie had never thought of doing before seemed almost second, or perhaps first, nature to her now. Before she realized what had happened, Ike's big hands were around her waist as he prepared to lift her down from the step. He held her for a moment, and she put her hands on his shoulders.

Was it to steady herself, or could it have been that she just wanted to feel his rough coat and the strength inside it? Ike must have misunderstood her action, for he pulled her up against his chest and suddenly bent his lips to hers.

Cassie was surprised—at Ike, rather than at herself, for she had become so forward since she met Ike that she had greatly wanted him to kiss her. Was this the carnal desire that Paul spoke about? Paul seemed to have a very poor opinion of it. Well, here was another case where Cassie believed that it might be better to judge from the spirit of the thing.

Ike set her down, his face shocked at the thing he had done. "Cassie, is thee angry with me? Thee is so little and so pretty. Thee sees, doesn't thee, that I could not contain myself? I meant thee no harm, Cassie."

Cassie was about to say, "It was not thy fault, Ike. I wanted thee to do it." But she realized that, even to reassure Ike that she did not mind, it might not be best to be so completely honest. Ike must already think her too forward to be maidenly.

Cassie managed to look a little shocked—as she was indeed—and felt again the warmth in her cheeks. She only hoped he would not jump to the conclusion that she really did mind!

Together they worked on the stack of wood, which now began to assume large proportions. Ike was stacking it so well that it would take more than a wandering cow to knock it down again.

It was plain that Ike was a thorough man, a little slow, but a good workman. Father would respect that. He wanted nothing slipshod. Even as forward-thinking as he was, Father found the new machine carving done on furniture displeasing, felt that it lacked the pride in workmanship found in good, hand-carved decoration.

Cassie made a great effort to bring a smile to Ike's face and was rewarded when a little of the solemnity began to leave. She would see that there was much merriment in their home, as much as there had been in her own. Would Ike want his child to be solemn?

Only, she wished to have many children, not just one. Would they have hair as red as hers, or—Cassie shut off the thought in alarm.

What had come over her, that she should be thinking such thoughts! Was there no limit to her unmaidenliness? The Friends in the meeting would say that it was caused by the books Father had permitted her to read, books that no careful father would allow in his home.

Now Cassie looked and saw the sun dipping low in the western sky. "Oh, Ike, it will be dark soon. I must go."

"Yes, thee must. I would not be the cause of thy being caught by nightfall. But how soon does thee think it would be fitting for me to come to speak to thy mother and thy father? Thee can see that it is hard for me to restrain my love for thee."

"Thee might come to the meeting on First Day, and thee could speak to my mother then and ask if thee might call at our home. My father will be gone for two weeks in the East."

"Thee thinks thy mother will not object?"

"My mother will like thee, thee may be sure."

"Thee says *thy mother* as if thee feared thy father might not. Does thee think thy father will find me lacking in worldly goods? Thee sees that I am not wealthy. But the little farm is mine, free from mortgage. We could live off it surely, though it would be very simple living. Would thee mind, Cassie?"

"No, Ike. I would be happy wherever thee is. The Spirit would not have sent thee to me unless it was right that we should be together. Father is different from many of the Friends. He would not wish thee to be wealthy; only that we should be happy together.

"But he might feel that we were not suited to each other," Cassie continued, trying hard to make plain to Ike her father's feeling in such matters. "Thee sees that I am of a lighter turn than thee, and Father will think of that. He would not want thee to find me different from what thee had in mind for a wife."

Suddenly afraid, Cassie asked, "Ike, thee would not want me to be different, to be a fine housewife, a fine tailor, would thee? Thee should know that I have not learned to milk a cow, or to make pants. I will learn if thee wishes, but thee must not expect too much at first. Father wished to teach me all that he had learned in college and in his reading. Thee would not have much use for Latin and Greek in thy little house, would thee, Ike?"

"Cassie, thee is perfect just as thee stands there. I would not have thee different in any way."

"Thee may not feel that way when thee sees what a poor shirt I will make. No doubt thee would not care for embroidery on thy work shirt. But I am better at embroidery than at plain sewing. I am not well grounded in housekeeping."

Ike's face clouded, and Cassie felt a great foreboding that the sisters in the meeting were right; no young man in moderate circumstance would wish to marry a girl who knew so few prac-

31

tical things. She listened with dread for his next remark.

"Thy father will not want thee to marry a man with so little worldly goods. If he did not wish thee to *learn* to do these things, he will be even less willing for thee to have them to do."

Cassie felt a great surge of relief. "Oh, no, Ike, that is not it. He just wanted me to be with him, and since I had no brothers and sisters, my mother was happy to do the things herself, since he felt so strongly about it. My mother loves my father so much that she wants him always to have the things he wants. There are other wives in the meeting who sometimes feel that Mother has spoiled Father, and so made it hard for them."

She continued, still fearfully, "Teaching school may not be good training for a wife. Now I am sorry I did not learn the things my mother could have taught me. Though, indeed, I can cook a good simple meal."

"Thee will learn what thee needs to know, never fear, little Cassie. Thee will not have to milk the cow, and thee sees that I am not a man who worries about his clothes or their style."

Cassie could see. But she could also see that she would want him to worry more about the style of his clothes. She thought fiercely that no one should laugh at Ike when he was her husband. She wanted other people to see Ike as she now saw him, not as she had seen him when first he had come to the meeting: all feet and long legs not adequately covered. It was queer how he had changed in her esteem in such a little while.

Not even the sun suddenly darkening in the west nor her urgent need to start home could make parting with Ike easy.

Ike seemed to sense her thoughts and asked, "Does thee want me to ride home with thee?"

"No, I am not afraid. And *thee* would just have to leave *me* if thee did that."

Ike helped her hitch the horse to the wagon, and Cassie reluctantly waved good-by as she turned the horse toward home.

After supper that evening, Cassie helped Mother with the dishes. When they were through, they sat down together beside the big fireplace, and Cassie said slowly, "Mother, does thee think thee could teach me to sew?"

"To sew, Cassie? Thee sews a fine seam very well. Does thee not like the dresses I make for thee? Thee has enough to do now with thy school without doing thy own sewing."

"But, Mother, does thee not think every girl should learn to make all manner of clothing? Thee knows I might someday have to make clothing for men. Thee has not taught me that at all."

"Thee will have time, Cassie. When thee begins to think of marriage, it will be time enough for that." It did seem that Mother looked at her with special attention as she said this.

Cassie said no more, but before she went to bed, she took down Father's big coat which hung in her closet and looked at it. It did look very hard. Of course Ike could buy his coats already made, but Cassie would surely have to make his everyday clothes from the brown jean. Her buttonholes alone were bad enough. What would a whole garment be like that she had made?

Of course, Mother could help her, but she would not like for Rachel or Priscilla Evans to speak slightingly of her ability to make clothes for Ike. Too, it would give the people in the meeting another reason to speak critically of her father.

⤙ VI ⤚

ON FIRST DAY MORNING THE SUN SHONE, AND THE FOREST WAS red with autumn colors as Cassie and her mother took the road to the meeting house. Since this road was not as good as the one

33

to the schoolhouse, they found it more pleasant to go by horseback than to drive the spring wagon.

"Mother, is my hair neat this morning?" Cassie asked as they went down the narrow road.

"Cassie, what is the matter with thee this morning? Thee has asked me four times if thee looks well. Thee looks well, of course. Thy hair is combed neatly, though the curls will slip from thy braids. Thy dress is modest and well-fitting. Thee is neat and clean, and that is all that is necessary in the sight of the Lord."

"Thank thee, Mother."

Cassie's glance was as quick as the little squirrel that jumped from tree to tree in the meeting house yard. Her eyes searched the hitching rack until she saw the horses of Wesley and Samuel Evans. Ike would be with them. One of them would certainly ask him over for the First Day meal, and he would not have to cook for himself today.

It was all she could do to sit with folded hands and quiet feet during the meeting. Even Mother seemed moved to speak at great length this morning.

This time Cassie believed that she could feel Ike's presence, and, indeed, it must have been so, for her glance flew to him without any seeking.

When meeting was at last over and everyone was leaving, Ike stepped away from his brothers and dropped in behind Cassie and her mother. Cassie spoke to him as they reached the outside of the meeting house. "Good morning, Ike Evans."

"Good morning, Cassie Ballinger, and Faith Ballinger."

Mother looked up quickly, surprised; then Cassie saw a look of understanding break over her mother's face. There was no use trying to hide things from Mother. No doubt she had wondered all week what was wrong with Cassie. Now she knew.

Ike helped them onto the upping block, holding their horses

as they mounted. Then he spoke gravely, respectfully. "Faith Ballinger, does thee mind if I call at thy house this evening to see thy daughter?"

Mother turned to Cassie and, when she saw Cassie's willing smile, said quite as gravely, "Thee would be most welcome, Ike Evans. Would thee care to join us for supper this evening? It will be a cold meal, for we do not eat heavily on First Day, but thee is welcome to share it with us."

Ike's face, usually so solemn, seemed somehow lighted from the inside. He looked almost handsome, not at all the sober young man who had been so frequently in Cassie's dreams.

As Ike rode away with his brothers and Mother and Cassie started down the narrow road, Mother looked at Cassie with a funny little smile. Cassie felt a great warmth of love for Mother who, without being told, could understand all the things that would have been so hard for her to say.

No doubt that was the reason Father had first loved Mother, who was so different from Father himself. Not that he was ever lacking for words to tell the things he thought. But it must have been very comforting to find someone who could understand lots of things without talking about them and somehow taking the shine off them.

With the thought of Father, the uneasiness that Cassie had been keeping in check began to grow. Father would not be so ready to accept her feeling for Ike and the plans they were about to make. It might be hard to make him understand. It was good that Mother would help her show him that being so different was not important.

Almost as though Mother had read her thoughts, she spoke. "Cassie, does thee think thy father will be pleased with thy young man?"

"How could he not be, Mother? Anyone can see that Ike is an admirable young man."

35

Mother's tone was dry. "That is true. But thee knows that thy father will expect more from any admirable young man who aspires to thy hand than most of the Friends."

Mother went on, her manner grave. "Thy father will want virtue; that is true. But he will also want learning, kindness, and humor. I fear there are few young men who could pass all the tests thy father will make for thy husband."

Cassie's spirits fell a little. She had had this in the back of her mind ever since Father had looked across the road at the little house and said, "A good young man, a little lacking in humor, but of a kinder turn than his brothers Samuel and Wesley." As a description of a brother of the Evanses, that was high praise indeed. But as a picture of a husband for Cassie, it left much to be desired in Father's eyes.

She had tried to keep the thought so far back in her mind that it need not bother her. If Cassie did not love Father so much, she would not worry whether he was pleased with the man she chose, for she knew that Father would not tell her that she could not marry Ike if she chose to do it.

But he could be deeply hurt when Cassie chose to do the things he thought unwise. And even though she would not willingly hurt Mother, somehow it seemed even harder for her to go deliberately against Father.

But Cassie's voice was firm as she answered, "Well, then, Mother, thee will just have to help me make Father understand that it is I who will be married to Ike, not Father. Indeed, it is Ike who could well complain of the way Father has allowed me to grow up without learning the housewifely skills that thee would have taught me." Her tone was a little indignant.

Mother was shocked. "Oh, Cassie, thee must not say these things. Already thee has put Ike Evans before thy father—has spoken unkindly of him, has reproached him for things thee once thought were as they should be. Oh, Cassie, thee will hurt him sharply!"

For almost the first time, Cassie realized that Mother must often have been hurt herself in these years when she had given up her daughter to the things that most fathers expect of their sons. Had her inability to bear more children, perhaps sons for Father, made this seem her duty? A new sense of sympathy came to Cassie.

How lonely it must have been for Mother to be deprived of teaching her daughter. Mother was so handy at doing all the things that made a wife respected in this country. But there were so few of these things that Cassie had learned.

From this new understanding Cassie spoke. "Thee has been hurt, too, Mother. Now I can see that thee has given me up to Father when thee could have taught me so many things. Thee could have used my help many times. Thee must often have felt that thy daughter was selfish and thoughtless with thee."

Mother's face had a sudden light on it that Cassie had never seen. She reached from her horse and laid her hand on Cassie's.

"No, Cassie, not that. Though there were many times when I did wish thee could be with both of us at the same time, learning both kinds of things. But I learned long ago that what thee cannot have, thee must accept. And ofttimes, as now, I have been amply repaid for my acceptance. Does thee understand?"

Cassie felt a queer tightness behind her eyes, as though she were about to cry. "Thee is good, Mother, thee is very good."

It was almost a relief to see that the gate was near. She could not tell Mother, but she would show her that she loved her quite as much as Father.

While Cassie put the horses away, Mother went into the house to set out the noon meal. The food had already been prepared on Seventh Day, for Mother would not often cook on

First Day—only if, as Father said, "the ox was in the ditch."

The chicken had been fried the day before; with it were stewed apples and tomatoes, which were not yet gone from the garden. The Ballingers had many vegetables that the other Friends did not think worth growing. Father Ballinger read many of the government bulletins and was forward-thinking, even in his garden.

As they sat down at the table, Cassie looked around the big kitchen and felt a little twinge of something very like homesickness. Her girlhood seemed to be slipping away from her. The cookstove of which Mother was so proud, the bureau with its marble top, the small drop-leaf table beside the big rocking chair, the whale-oil lamp which Father had so recently brought from the East, the large table at which they ate their meals, and the ladderback chairs in which they were now seated—all at once these things seemed not to be hers, but only Mother's and Father's. It was as if she were already gone.

Now she must begin to think of what she would have in her own home, hers and Ike's.

They bowed their heads in a silent grace and then began their meal.

"Mother, does thee think we should be adding to my chest? It would be nice if Father were to bring me something from his trip."

"Yes, Cassie, but thee knows thy father is more like to bring thee a book than a silver spoon."

Cassie's loyalty to Father made her speak up for him now. "Thee knows, Mother, that until now I preferred that Father bring me a book. It will be a blow to Father, truly."

"Thy father has always known that someday thee would find a husband."

"Yes, Mother, but thee is right that Ike is not the husband he

38

would have chosen. He would not choose for me to be a pioneer, even though he himself was one, and thee."

"No, but thy father is a reasonable man. He will soon be able to laugh at his unwillingness for thee to do as he himself did when he left his home in the East for a harder life. It will be hard for him, for thee is the apple of his eye. But he will soon see."

Cassie smiled gratefully at her mother. The shadow that had for a little obscured her joy in this new happiness was lifted.

Was Ike as happy and stirred as she? Would he be able to keep his feeling from his brothers and their families, who would be quick to sense any change in his attitude? Cassie hoped he would be circumspect, for she wanted Father to know of this before Ike's brothers. And it would be several days before Father would return.

They washed up the few dishes they had used, and Cassie hung the dishcloth on the line outside. She looked down the dirt road with the grass growing between the tracks, wondering how soon Ike would feel that he could come. He must be quite as anxious as she; she would not believe he could be less so.

In a flurry of anticipation, Cassie hurried into the house, straightened a chair, fluffed a pillow, and pulled the hooked rug to a line more parallel with the table before which it lay. She was glad that she had made a hooked rug this last summer to put in her chest with the sheets and pillow slips, the knitted lace, and the tatting that Mother had made for her down through the years.

Mother Ballinger was soon seated beside the little table with her worn copy of the Holy Scriptures. Cassie chose a work of George Fox, tried to seat herself as calmly and decorously as her mother, then remembered that she was seventeen to her mother's thirty-seven. Switching to the copy of the Holy Scrip-

39

tures that her father had brought her when she was ten, she turned to the Song of Solomon.

Father had once said that no more beautiful love songs had ever been written and that he himself felt that Solomon had done a greater thing in this work than in building the temple. Bricks and stones could be destroyed, but not words in a man's mind. Mother had been sitting on the other side of the room as Father said this, and Cassie had been surprised to see a flush rise above Mother's ears and spread until it covered her whole face. Until then Cassie had not thought that her mother was really young—young and very lovely. That had been two years ago, and Father's words had meant little to Cassie, only a matter of curiosity. Now she felt some of Mother's warmth as she read these songs.

Would Ike ever say such things to her? No—the answer to that was not hard. Ike would never even read these words to her. If he read them at all, it would be in the light of prophecy, of that she was sure—not as though they could ever apply to real flesh and blood people.

A little flicker of uneasiness went over Cassie. Would she ever be sorry that she had chosen a husband who would ignore the thought that the man who had written these words had loved a woman, as the words expressed? Yet Ike had kissed her when she had wished him to. Perhaps she would find other things in Ike that she did not expect.

She quickly told herself that Ike's virtues more than made up for any lack there might be in him. Briefly as she had known him, she was sure that Ike could never be cruel to her, never be anything but patient and kind, completely good. Ike could answer all the queries at the meeting as they were supposed to be answered—queries and answers she had heard for so many years that they sometimes seemed only words without any meaning. Just looking into Ike's face told her that to Ike they were more than mere words. They were commands to be obeyed.

All the meetings for worship and discipline would be attended. Unbecoming behavior in the meeting would be guarded against (even the smile that she had given him that First Day). He would have Christian love toward his brothers (even when they were Wesley and Samuel).

They would endeavor to bring up their children in Christian principles and in plainness and simplicity. Ike would guard his children from reading pernicious books (Would Ike's definition of pernicious books be the same as hers?) and from corrupt conversation. He would encourage them to read the Holy Scriptures diligently (but not the Song of Solomon).

Ike would surely see that the Holy Scriptures were used as a class book in all the schools his children attended and that portions thereof were read daily by the teacher.

If at any time Cassie herself should do something that Ike thought was wrong, he would surely deal with her seasonably and impartially. He would endeavor to evince to her, if she would not be reclaimed, the spirit of meekness and love before he placed judgment upon her.

Ike would maintain a testimony against priests, ministers' wages, slavery, oaths, and lotteries, and against bearing arms and all military service and trading in goods taken in war.

Ike would see that they were careful to live within the bounds of their circumstances and to avoid involving themselves in business beyond their ability to manage or in hazardous or speculative trade. He would be punctual in complying with their engagements and in paying their debts seasonably.

All these things Cassie had heard from her youth up, in the questions and responses in the meetings. The words were as familiar to her as her own name, and she knew they must be to Ike also.

But Cassie had been taught that the spirit was more important than the rules themselves. Had Ike? Or would Ike someday think that she was not a good Friend? Cassie knew herself to be too much like Father ever to pretend to believe anything with which she could not agree, even though it was in the rules of the Friends' discipline. Might she sometime bring shame upon Ike by doing something that would cause the committee to call upon her and remonstrate with her?

But, of course, love would take care of all these things. If Ike should be narrow in some things, life with Cassie would broaden him. Cassie laughed aloud. Mother raised her eyes from the Scriptures and looked at her questioningly.

"What is thee laughing at, my child?"

"At Ike Evans, and how life with me would broaden him."

Mother smiled a little doubtfully. "Yes, my child, it would. Life with thy father has been a broadening influence on me. No doubt thee, too, will change thy partner, and for the better. But remember, Cassie, thee cannot expect Ike to do all the changing. Thee must try to see his point of view as well as thine own. Marriage is a partnership affair."

Cassie nodded. "I know, Mother. I was thinking that I must be careful to be a good wife to Ike. But thee knows that if Ike is thinking in error about some things, it will be my duty to witness for the truth with him."

"Yes, Cassie, but thee must be very sure that it is God's truth, not thine, when thee witnesses."

Cassie's thoughts were grave as she considered her mother's words. It was a relief to escape from these thoughts and a joy to hear Ike's horse turn into the lane toward the house.

⤙ VII ⤛

It was hard to be maidenly and not run to open the door, to hurry out to greet Ike. He would surely be as glad to see Cassie as she to see him; but it was, of course, not fitting for her to show her eagerness in his first call.

But they had already progressed far beyond the first call.

However, she would yield to custom in things so unimportant as these. So Cassie sat modestly until she heard his knock at the door. She could not resist a little skip in her steps as she hurried to open it.

"Will thee come in?"

"Thank thee, Cassie."

Mother rose to greet Ike and showed him the chair in which Father always sat. This alone told Cassie all she needed to know as to whether Mother found him as admirable as she did. One had only to look at Ike to see his virtue. That was clear!

To Cassie's surprise, she could think of nothing important enough to say now that Ike was here. And Ike sat in growing soberness. This would be a sober occasion to Ike.

Cassie didn't want it to be sober! This was the happiest thing that had ever happened to either of them. She wouldn't let it be spoiled by unnatural solemnity—unnatural at least as far as Cassie was concerned.

"How is thy cow, Ike? The one who wanders."

Cassie had no sooner said these words than she knew that she should not have said them. She had taken a happening that should have belonged to them alone and made it a matter of public conversation, even though it was only before her mother. Ike's face was hurt, and Cassie would have bitten her tongue, if it would have helped.

She turned to her mother and said quickly, "Ike's cow sometimes wanders away, and he has to hunt for her."

There was gratitude on Ike's face.

Then what could she say? How could she make Ike smile? Was he to smile only when they were alone and no one could see his faltering levity? Had life been so unkind to Ike before he met her? She would somehow make up to him for all the years before he had known her.

Cassie suddenly thought of a way to take him out of the house into the sunshine. "Would thee care to see the new puppies we have? Our dog is very proud of them. Thee could have one to keep thee company if thee wished. Thee must be very lonely in thy house with no one to be with thee."

At the realization of what she had said, Cassie felt herself becoming warm and surely blushing again. What a thing for her to say! Ike would think her very bold.

From under lowered lashes, she looked at him and saw the slow smile which was as much a part of the Ike she loved as his preternatural solemnity. It began in his eyes and ended on his long upper lip. And it gave a very knowing and merry look to his sober countenance.

"Thee is right. It is very lonely. Though only in these last few weeks have I found it so. I am not a man who needs company in general."

"Thee does not think a puppy would help?"

"Let us go and see them. It might be that one would take a liking to me, so that he would not be lonely for his mother."

With a sympathetic smile, Mother watched them go out the door. She would understand that it could be hard for them to speak before other people when they knew each other so little —and yet so much.

"Thy mother will not think it amiss that we leave her?"

"Mother will know that thee will protect me."

44

"Does thee think thy mother will believe thee needs protection?"

"More like she will think thee will need the protection!"

Ike's face was a study in bewilderment, and Cassie wondered what perversity made her say such things.

"What does thee mean, Cassie?"

"Ike, when thee is solemn there is a spirit in me that makes me say things to shock thee. Thee must not think I am being serious. I am only trying to make thee smile. But thee sees that I am a forward young woman, determined to steal thee away from all the other young women who would like to have thee call on them this First Day afternoon!"

"Thee knows, Cassie, there is no one but thee that I would want to keep me from being lonely. Thee does not need to tease me. Though we are yet so strange to each other, it seems to me that I have been waiting for thee always. Does thee feel so too?"

"Yes, Ike, thee sees that I do."

Becky had her family in a corner of the old log barn, which Father had saved when he built the new one. The puppies were big enough to come running to meet Cassie, and she knew that Father would soon say they must all be given away. Ike could have his choice.

"Which does thee think would be best for thee, Ike?"

Ike stooped down and picked up a little black one, and it snuggled up to his shirt.

"This seems a likely one, Cassie. Would thee be willing for me to take this one?"

Cassie saw that Ike was a man who knew how to deal with animals and who did not hesitate when there were decisions to make. The puppy seemed to realize that Ike would be kind to him.

"Thee may have any thee chooses. Will thee let it stay in the house with thee?"

45

"My mother always says a dog should stay out of doors, that the house is not a place for a dog."

"But thee, Ike? What does thee think? Thy mother will not be with thee, so if thee chooses, thee can have it in the house with thee. We let Becky come in the house when she does not have puppies. A dog would be company for thee."

Ike's face clouded. Would he insist that their life be run as his mother had run the life of her family?

Now he said with decision, "I think thee is right, Cassie. It would be very companionable, having thy puppy in the house with me. What does thee think we should name him?"

Cassie pondered a little. It seemed somehow important that they choose a name that would have some humorous reference, not just a name to be naming, as was often the custom. Farmers seemed to name their animals for the people from whom they were purchased, and this seemed shirking a pleasant duty.

Cassie said, "I think thee should either name an animal because it seems fitting for that particular animal, or find some name that has a special meaning for thee, thyself."

Cassie looked into the puppy's face. "Does thee know, Ike, I see a little resemblance to Elder Nicholson. Does thee think we might name him Nick?"

If Cassie had expected Ike to object on the ground of respect to the elder, she was pleasantly surprised. There was a twinkle in Ike's eye as he said gravely, "There *is* a resemblance—a somewhat owlish look about them both. A good idea, Cassie!"

Cassie felt a great lift of spirit. There would be things they could laugh about together. And when Ike was too sober, Nick would be a reminder that, if she persevered, she could occasionally find Ike's streak of humor.

"Let us go back and look for bittersweet, Ike. Father said there would be some on the back rail fence. We will leave Nick with Becky until thee is ready to go home."

When they came to the first fence, Ike climbed over and, reaching up, lifted Cassie over beside him. Cassie hoped he would not set her down at once, but be tempted as he had been on the steps of the schoolhouse. But perhaps he remembered that they could be seen from Mother's window. There would be other fences. Strange, but it seemed to be natural for Cassie to recognize these temptations, even before they appeared.

They walked through the field beside the corn waiting to be cut and shocked. Cassie had always liked autumn, but never with such joy as this. Ahead of them was the fence laden by bittersweet with its red berries.

They began to break the branches, but Ike said, "I think there are prettier ones on the other side of the fence. May I help thee over?"

So, Ike could think of these things, too.

Again Ike climbed over, and Cassie stepped on the lower rail. He lifted her up and over, then stood with her in his big hands. Was it her fault, or did Ike pull her a little closer? Suddenly, without any intention on her part, Cassie's arms were around his neck, and Ike was kissing her hungrily. And she was returning his kisses with quite as much fervor.

"Cassie, Cassie, thee is so little and so sweet. How could thee love a big lumbering creature like me?"

Cassie drew back from him angrily. "Don't ever say such things, Ike Evans! Thee is not a big lumbering creature. Do not belittle thyself. Thee is a fine figure of a man, as anyone can see."

Ike drew her closer to him and gazed into her eyes. "Oh, Cassie, I never thought to find anyone like thee to love me."

"Well, now, Ike, what did thee expect?"

Still holding her, Ike walked over to a log, which lay along the side of the field. He seated himself and placed Cassie on his lap, holding her close.

He was silent a moment, then said, "How could I believe that thee would be happy with what I can offer thee? Thee can see that I have little in the way of worldly goods. Only what thee could see at my little farm."

"Does thee think I would marry a man for the money he would have?"

"But, Cassie, what will thy father say? Thee says thyself that he did not want thee to learn to do many of the things that thee would have to do if thee should marry me. Will he forbid thee to marry me, or at least oppose thy marriage?"

Cassie answered slowly, "I will tell thee honestly, Ike. Father will not wish me to marry thee—or anyone—at first. For Father will not want me to leave home. Thee sees, my father is not like other men. But Ike, thee will be cheated in thy wife. In thy situation, thee will need a wife who knows how to make thy clothes, to milk a cow and raise chickens. I will learn, but no doubt thy mother will think thee should find a wife who already knows how to do these things."

Ike only held her closer. "Thee is a logical young lady, but thee need not worry about my thinking I am cheated. If thee is willing to get along until I can give thee a better house—and someday I will, I promise thee—I will be patient until thee learns the things thee must know."

"So long as we have each other, it will not trouble us, will it, Ike?"

Ike put his big hands around Cassie's face and bent to kiss her. Truly this Ike Evans belied his slow and ordered manner! It was Cassie, shaken, who pulled herself out of his arms and stood trembling before him.

"I think we had best go back to the house. Mother will wonder what has happened to us."

She straightened the red curls which had escaped the braids

coiled at her neck. Standing on tiptoe, she kissed Ike gently. "Does thee think me forward, Ike?"

"I think thee was meant to be my wife, Cassie. Thee will not make me wait long, will thee?"

"Only so long as Father says we must wait. I could not hurt him by going against his will in that. But he is good to me; he will not delay us, I am sure. And the school must be taught for this term; that thee knows."

Ike's voice was a little concerned. "I am worried about thy father's feeling in this, Cassie. I cannot see how he would give thee to me. He must have aimed much higher for thee."

"Ike, thee will have to quit belittling thyself, or I will not marry thee! Thee knows that, as Friends, we do not hold any man higher than another, except as he bears himself in goodness."

"Thee is right, Cassie. No doubt I am a better man than I thought, or thee would not find me satisfactory to thee. I begin to see that I must be as good as thee says! There, does thee like that?"

"That is better! And thee must not let Father overawe thee, either!"

⊰ VIII ⊱

THE NEXT WEEK WENT MORE QUICKLY THAN ANY CASSIE HAD ever known. She longed for Father's return, yet dreaded it. She wished to share her happiness, yet knew it would not be happiness for him. Cassie feared he would oppose their plans at first and so take some of her joy away. Yet she trusted Father's love enough to believe that, when he understood, he would agree. But how could she make him understand?

Every day after the children were gone, Ike came to the door and spoke to her. Never did he come into the building, for he feared he would harm her good name if someone were to say that he met her here in the empty schoolhouse. Then her father might well have cause to disapprove of his actions.

On Fourth Day evening, Ike came and accompanied Cassie and her mother to the midweek meeting. When they returned, Cassie wanted him to stay and visit, but he said she must not be tired for her next day's work. It was good to have him wish to care for her, to protect her.

Cassie looked ahead, and it seemed that the term would be long. She almost wished that she had not begun to teach; but if she had not, would she have found Ike so quickly? If she had not been forced to go and get him to remove his cow, his sisters-in-law would have chosen Sara Newby for him before he could meet Cassie and find that she was the wife for him! Yet this could not be true, for when one followed the Light, things worked out for one's good. And Ike was for her good. She said a prayer of thanks to God for his goodness.

On Sixth Day Mother made the mince turnovers that Father liked so well, dressed a chicken for frying, and made salt rising bread. Father would be home on Seventh Day.

Ike must come over on First Day and ask him for her hand. But before that, Cassie would have fought the battle and won it for him. Father had never yet been able to refuse Cassie any good thing, and he must see that Ike was good.

At last it was time for Father to come. Cassie watched from the window. There came the light wagon he had driven to the railroad station and left in the livery stable there. As the horse neared the house, it began to gallop, and Cassie thought it was as impatient to be home as Father himself.

While Mother watched from the doorway, Cassie, as always, ran out the door and met him with a hug, then stood back to look at him as Caleb, the hand, came and took the horse to the barn.

"Thee has been gone a long time, Father, yet thee has changed but little."

Dear Father. Cassie had thought that she would find a husband like him, but surely there was little resemblance. Father was not very tall, though his high-crowned beaver hat made him look taller. He was not heavy, but well-fleshed, with broad shoulders under his black coat. His fine white shirt was little mussed from the ride, for Father carried himself with a dignity that did not allow his clothes to be mussed. But beneath the dignity was a ready smile, a jolliness Cassie greatly loved and admired.

Father looked at her closely. "Now thee has changed, my Cassie. What has happened to thee? Thee is even prettier than thee was when I left."

With one hand holding his carpetbag, the other around her shoulders, he went with her up the flagstone walk. Cassie did not answer his question but walked with her arm around him to meet Mother at the door.

Now Cassie recognized that, glad as Father was to see her, he was even happier to see Mother. As he put his bag on the floor and took Mother in his arms, Cassie, suddenly tactful, picked up the bag and took it to her parents' room, leaving Father to greet Mother in privacy. Never had she thought before that, even as old as her parents were, they could wish to be alone. Being in love did give a person understanding.

Mother's face was pink as she and Father came into the bedroom where Cassie was unpacking his bag. Father's voice was teasing. "Looking to see what thy father brought thee, is thee?"

From one corner of the bag, he brought out two packages

and handed one to Cassie and one to Mother. Cassie unwrapped the white paper and folded it to put away for later use. This was a nicer paper than the stores in Greenbury had. Her hands shook a little as she opened the package. Father always brought such nice gifts, but recently Cassie's tastes had changed. Yet nothing could have been more welcome than the gift she found. Inside was a long length of grey silk.

"Oh, Father, thank thee! It is beautiful."

Mother's piece was black and would be very nice for her dark hair, but Cassie knew that no color, no matter how far it might depart from plainness, could be more becoming to her bright red hair than the grey. Father had once said, "Thee cannot seem very plain in thy dress, Cassie, thee is so flaming in thy hair."

After dinner, Father told Mother how much better her cooking was than the food in the inns where he had stopped. Cassie insisted that Mother sit down with Father while she washed the dishes. For once, Mother seemed willing to allow Cassie to do the work and so allow her to be with her husband.

A sudden thought struck Cassie; it might be that Mother would enjoy the extra time she would have with Father when Cassie was married and in her own home. That would be only natural, and Cassie did not mind the thought at all. Not now.

When the dishes were finished and the floor swept, Cassie joined Mother and Father beside the little table where Mother had lighted the oil lamp.

"Now, Father, tell us what thee did while thee was gone. Whom did thee see?"

For two hours Father talked, for Father liked to talk, and he had many things to tell. He had been to Yearly Meeting and had met many of the Friends, and many who were relatives as well.

Always before, Cassie had been quite as willing to listen as Father was to tell of his trips. But this time she had to guard her tongue lest she interrupt to speak of Ike, to mention something Ike had told her about the meetings he had attended when he was a young boy and had gone with his father to Philadelphia.

At last Father said, "Now, daughter, what news has thee? How goes the school? Has thee had trouble with any of thy pupils?"

"The school, Father? Oh, all goes well. The students are very good and well-behaved. I read the Holy Scriptures every day in the class."

"Thee seems to have something else on thy mind, Cassie." He looked at her sharply, and she felt the warm flush rising in her face.

"Has thee met a young man, Cassie?"

"Yes, Father." She had always been honest with Father. She could not equivocate now.

"Tell me, Cassie, who is this young man? Surely not one of thy pupils!"

Cassie had gone over and over in her mind just how she would tell him. First she would tell him that an admirable young man wished to marry her. She would describe all the good things about Ike, and, after she had prejudiced him in Ike's favor, then she would tell him his name. But under Father's shrewd glance, she could only answer straightforwardly.

"Ike Evans, Father, the young man across from my school."

Father's voice held astonishment, dismay, and something she would not believe could be scorn. "Cassie, thee does not mean the brother of Samuel and Wesley Evans? Thee surely does not mean that young man, that mournful young man."

"Yes, Father." She made her voice steady, firm. "But he is not mournful, only quiet. And thee knows thee thyself would not like a loud young man."

It was all as bad as Cassie had feared, perhaps even worse: the hurt on Father's face, the disappointment. Cassie suddenly felt herself grown up and alone, already cut off from Father and his approval.

She knew him so well, knew that when Father's hands were clamped firmly on the arms of the big chair it was because he was fighting to control his impulse to speak plainly, perhaps with too much emphasis. But to have Father look at her with such doubt and reproach! Only her love for Ike could make her strong enough to disregard the pleading in Father's face.

At last he spoke with great reasonableness and a kind of certitude she would not accept. "Thee will find many young men, Cassie, now that thee has found that young men can be of interest to thee."

"No, Father. No other young man. I wish to marry Ike, and he wishes to marry me. Thee has taught me to think for myself, to know when the thing I wish to do is through the leading of the Light."

Father's face fell; she saw him struggle with himself, saw him look at her carefully to see if this was really a serious thing. Father had treated her as an adult too long to feel free to say that she thought as a child. His smile was a difficult one, for him and for his daughter who loved him.

"When will he be here to talk to thy father as would be fitting? More fitting than to speak to thee first."

Cassie laughed, but kindly. "Father, thee should know that thy daughter would not forget that thee has often said thee and Mother had thy plans all made before thee asked her father for her hand."

Father smiled in answer, but it was a tight little smile, not like Father's usual one at all. "Thee remembers too much, my daughter. But thee must know that this young man will have to be a very fine and unusual young man before I will give thee to him. Very different from his brothers."

"Father, thee knows I could not wish to marry one like his brothers."

Then she spoke almost sharply. "Father, thee is not one to make up thy mind without knowing of what thee speaks. Thee knows thee cannot judge a man by his brothers. Thee says thyself that some of thy own brothers are not as thee would have them."

"Thee is right, my child. I will withhold judgment until I know thy young man better."

"He will come to see thee tomorrow, Father."

There was a kind of constraint about the remainder of the evening that hurt Cassie sorely. She could not give up Father when she became Ike's wife. Of course it would be different then, but she would not allow Father to be taken away from her. Nor, she thought grimly, would she allow Father to take Ike away from her.

The next morning Cassie rode to meeting behind her father on his horse. When they reached the meeting house yard, he pulled his horse beside the upping block and, reaching behind him, swung Cassie down. She looked around quickly to see if Ike had arrived.

Down the road she saw him approaching on a tall roan mare. He rode handsomely, and Cassie was proud. She would have liked to wait and go in and sit beside him, had it not been for the partition.

Cassie sat quietly through the service. It seemed longer than any she had ever attended. Her mind would not stay on thoughts of God as she wished. But surely God would understand.

When at last the service was over, they filed slowly out of the little meeting house. Ike came over to them, and Mother said sweetly, "Father, this is Friend Ike Evans."

Surely Ike could not sense the disapproval in Father's voice as he greeted Ike. But Cassie recognized a tightness in Father's lips, an overly appraising glance he did not usually bestow upon new acquaintances. Indeed, it was like the measuring glances of Samuel and Wesley Evans, though it held more sweetness, more of the spirit of Christian love.

They rode three abreast down the country road. Father spoke pleasantly of the beauty of the day, of the goodly number at meeting, and of the merits of the sermon. Ike answered with dignity and respect, and Cassie was proud: proud of his height, of his upright bearing, proud of everything about him but his solemnity. Father might almost think him dour.

When they reached the house, Ike helped Cassie down from her father's horse and then accompanied Father to the barn, where they must bed, feed, and water the horses even though it was First Day.

Father seemed completely unlike his usual friendly self, and Cassie wished that she could somehow make these two men understand each other, since she loved them both so much. Mother kept the conversation going, and Cassie tried to draw Ike out, to lead him to say the things that would make Father see him for what he was. But Ike would not be led. He was proper and polite, but not very amusing company.

To be sure, Ike had probably been brought up to believe that one should not be amusing on First Day. Yet Cassie had found him most entertaining last First Day when they looked for bittersweet.

Cassie knew that, if Father wished, he could put Ike at ease, could make him say the things that would make him seem a more interesting young man. But she could see that Father had no intention of putting Ike in any better light than Ike placed himself. He didn't really want Ike to be put in a good light. He wanted him to seem a dull young man, to compare very unfavorably with himself when it came to being interesting to Cassie.

Cassie didn't usually become vexed with Father, but now she seemed to catch fire from the flame in her hair. She could almost feel a burning inside her, one that started slowly but gained in intensity. Father could not do that to Ike; she would not let him.

Cassie turned to Father, looked him sharply in the eye, and said clearly, but with a sweetness Father would understand if Ike did not, "Father, why doesn't thee tell Ike about thy life when thee first went to Ohio, about the first house thee and Mother had to live in? About how different it was then from the way it is now when thee has been married so much longer and has had a chance to make things easier for thy family?"

Father looked at Cassie. And all at once he seemed to realize how he had been acting, how hard he had been making it for Cassie, and for Ike. Then, with a little gesture that signified his defeat, he said, "Thee knows, Cassie, it was a different age."

"Yes, Father, but thee, too, was a different age. Thee has told me that when thee was young, thee had things very hard. Thee remembers that, but thee would like for thy child to start where thee left off. Does thee think it such a good thing, not to struggle for the good things in life? Thee has said sometimes that it is not the things we have but the struggle we have to get them that makes them worthwhile."

"Thee has a good memory, child. Better, perhaps, than thee will have when thee is my age."

"Thee does not seem so old to me, William Ballinger," Ike said. "I have heard that thee has very young and up-to-date ideas. Thee keeps abreast of the times, and I think thy daughter is much like thee."

57

Father smiled with pleasure. "Does thee, Ike Evans?" Then, warningly he added, "Thee may find also that her likeness to her father may cause thee trouble. Her mother sometimes finds my young and up-to-date ideas bringing the committee to our door."

Ike said steadily, "That is of no great importance so long as there is clearness that it is God's will. After all, the committee is formed of men, and their judgments are only human. And Friends do not obey the will of the committee, but the will of God."

Father looked at Ike with new respect. "Thee is right, Ike Evans. I have often told Cassie's mother that I am not answerable to the committee for my actions."

Mother smiled and said, "Yes, William, but there are times when thee is apt to mistake *thy* will for God's."

Father looked at her reproachfully, "When I have thee to point this out, we often avoid the call from the committee."

The rest of the day went well. After dinner was over, Ike looked at Father and said very simply, "William Ballinger, I know that thee must think there could be no one worthy of thy daughter. I think thee is right. But I love her, and would like thy permission to ask her to marry me."

Father laughed kindly and said, "Ike Evans, I think thee is a bit late in asking my permission. Cassie has already asked me, or it would be more truthful to say *told* me, just as so often happens. And since there would be no use in my saying no, since she has made up her mind, I can only say that I will be glad to have thee for a son."

Father's way of saying it was more gracious than the words he used, and Cassie felt relieved. To be sure, Father would still have his doubts about their suitability for each other, but he would not oppose them after this.

⤙ IX ⤚

CASSIE HAD NOT THOUGHT SIX MONTHS COULD BE SO LONG. THERE was, however, much to do, much to get ready, and much to learn. Plain sewing she would learn as she worked on the things to put in her chest.

But still there was the dreadful thought of the clothing she must learn to make for Ike: the pants and waistcoats, the drawers, and the socks she must knit for him. So long as Mother had the time, Cassie knew that she would be glad to knit for him. But what wife would allow her mother to knit her husband's socks, simply because she did not know how? Cassie could easily make a shawl, but to turn the toe and heel of a sock—that she must learn.

It was hard to do her school work and still have time for the things she must learn—and to find time for the most important thing of all: seeing Ike when he came to call. Cassie had never before had to hurry to get done the things that must be done. Father's lessons had been easy for her, and Mother's requirements light. This hurrying in itself was a new experience.

Mother said that it might be good for her to find out how it would be if she had the large family she wished and there were more things to do than she could find time for. This might be good training.

Mother taught her to make lye soap with wood ashes and to make candles, for it was not likely that Ike could afford a sperm-oil lamp and its fuel, such as the Ballingers used. Cassie would willingly have learned to spin and weave, if it had seemed that she would need this knowledge.

Father wavered between an anxious look he tried to hide and a great willingness to buy many things for the house—things

Cassie would not allow him to buy. Once Cassie overheard Mother say, "Thee knows, William, it is not likely that Ike will wish to be beholden to thee in so many things. Thee knows that a man of parts will wish to do these things for himself and his wife."

Father knew that this was true and did not make an issue of it, but Cassie could see how it hurt him to think that she would not have the things she was used to. And Father seemed to feel a guiltiness for not having allowed Mother to teach her the things the neighboring women had taught their daughters, making it harder for Cassie than it should have been. It was a hard time for Father too.

Ike had written to the clerk of the meeting in southern Indiana where his membership was and had received a recommendation that he be admitted to membership in the meeting his brothers attended. Then he had written of his marriage plans to his mother and father and had told his brothers and their families.

At last Ike and Cassie sat on the facing bench and put their intention to marry before the meeting. A committee was appointed to inquire after Cassie's "clearness relative to marriage engagements with others." This seemed a little odd to Cassie, though she had heard the words so expressed all her life. There had never been a young man who interested her enough for her to enter into any kind of engagement with him.

And here was Ike, with no more learning, no more prospects, and—if Father was right—no more admirable traits than several young men in the meeting, young men who seemed not at all admirable to Cassie.

But Father and Ike had become good friends. Father had a great amount of time on his hands just now, and he had gone over and helped Ike with some carpentry work around the house and barn. This he did very tactfully, pretending that he would need the horse that Cassie drove to school, but lingering after he brought her and coming for her hours before she was ready. Father had helped build more than one pioneer church and school and had taken part in many "raisings," so he could teach Ike much. Cassie was pleased to glance out the schoolroom window and see Father and Ike mending the chicken-yard fence while the puppy, Nick, got underfoot.

One evening Father said with a considering air, "Thy young man seems a very likely fellow. He works hard and learns with ease. Thee will have a snug place when he is finished with it. If only thee would let me—"

"Father," Cassie interrupted, "thee must not worry about what thee cannot do for me. Thee sees that Ike is all I want."

"If thee would but let me have a well dug for thee, Cassie, I would not ask to do anything else. Thee will need a well badly, and Ike will be busy with the clearing of the new fields and the other work that must be done. It will be long before he will find time to dig thee a well. Now, if the well at the schoolhouse were good, thee could get water from there. It will be a long time before thee has thy own." Father was not one who liked repetition, but Cassie could see that he wanted emphasis in this.

She answered him quickly, but with a tender smile. "Then he will carry water for me from the Elliotts'. They will not care. They have already told him he is welcome to the water. Ike will not want to be beholden to thee."

So Father had to be content with getting things for Cassie that she would not really need, things like thin, coin-silver spoons. It was queer how a father could spend so much more for something a daughter did not need, and the husband-to-be not mind, while if he were to put half that much money into something she really needed, the husband's pride must suffer. It was not truly logical.

But Cassie liked the smooth feel of the spoons, and Ike could look at them with pleasure. Samuel's and Wesley's wives had a wistfulness in their gaze when she showed them the spoons. The Evans brothers did not feel that such spoons were needful; they felt that it would be better to buy more land for grain, though they did appreciate the thought that the pure silver would never wear out.

The meeting gave its approval to the marriage, but Cassie wondered if Samuel and Wesley might have their doubts. Then a committee was appointed to "attend the marriage and entertainment, if there be any, and see that good order is observed."

Father could at least buy Cassie a wedding dress, a new bonnet, and a shawl. This shawl was the finest Cassie had ever seen. She was a little afraid that a committee might come to remonstrate with Father for his extravagance, though no one could say that it was not "within the bounds of his circumstances." Though so fine, it was a very plain and simple shawl, with no adornment.

Cassie waited for Ike's mother to write her a letter welcoming her into the family—but waited in vain. Wesley and Samuel came to call with their wives and were very cordial. They made Cassie feel that, though they could not always agree with Father, they thought him a man worthy of respect, a man whose daughter any family would be glad to have join with their brother in marriage. Samuel's wife, Priscilla, who was somewhat given to talking, said to Cassie in passing, "Thee must not expect Ike's mother to write to thee. She is not one to engage in idle words, to speak of what she does not know in fact. She will not tell thee she is glad for Ike to marry thee until she can see thee and judge if thee will make him a good wife."

She added comfortingly, "But Rachel and I have written to tell her that thee is a fine girl and of a good family, and that the meeting has approved thy marriage."

This was a little frightening to Cassie. Surely Mother Evans could have found words to show her kindly intention without committing herself to approval. It might be well that Mother Evans was so far away from where Ike and Cassie would live.

Cassie did not repeat this conversation to Father, knowing he would be very much vexed for anyone to believe that Cassie was not more than Ike had a right to expect. Logic did not always affect Father when it came to his daughter.

One evening Ike said a little doubtfully that they might go on a short trip after the ceremony and visit his mother. He suggested it, not as though he found pleasure in the thought, but as though he felt it a duty. Yet Ike left the decision to Cassie.

Her answer was thoughtful. "Does thee think it would be a happy way to celebrate our marriage?"

His expression was all the answer she needed. She answered the look without waiting for his words, words she knew he did not wish to speak. "Let us just stay in thy little house and become acquainted before I meet thy mother. Later we will go to see her, Ike."

The relief on his face told her a great deal more than he would have told her, or could have told her if he had tried.

Cassie and her mother spent some time at Ike's house doing the chores that women think must be done, though it was already as clean as soap and scrubbing could make it. The small-paned windows with their wavy glass, the wooden floor waiting for the rugs from Cassie's chest, the cookstove which Ike had polished until Cassie was able to see her face in it were all ready.

At last it was time for school to end, and the pupils and parents made a pitch-in dinner for Cassie to show how they felt about her teaching. One of the older girls read a composition she had written for the whole school, telling of their great admiration and respect for Cassie.

There was a great lump in Cassie's throat as she tried to tell them how glad she was that she had taught, even if only for the one year. She thought with wonder that, when school opened again, she would already have been married for months. Life moved very quickly sometimes, at least when one looked back and saw the part that was already done.

THE WEDDING WAS TO BE HELD ON FIRST DAY AT TWO O'CLOCK. On that day, Cassie was ready early. She wore her new grey dress with a white kerchief at the neck, a bonnet made by a mantua-maker in Greenbury, and the cashmere shawl. As she looked at Mother and Father, she could see tears in their eyes.

Suddenly Cassie felt a great homesickness for the life and the home she was leaving. Father was right. She was very young. Did she really know Ike well enough to leave all this loved and familiar life to go and live with him in the house across from her school?

If Cassie should say she had changed her mind, Father would surely be glad, would take her and Mother with him to the East until her action was a little forgotten here. But he would also be ashamed, as would Mother. And Ike—he would then truly be a mournful young man!

As if she knew Cassie's thoughts, Mother kissed her gently and said, "Thee will be fine, Cassie. All will be well."

Then Father became cheerful and said, "Thee is bringing us a good son—something we have always longed for. We are happy for thee, for Ike, and for ourselves."

As they drew up in front of the meeting house, Ike was outside waiting. Cassie knew the meeting house was filled with their friends and relatives. The committee appointed to observe the wedding and its conduct was already inside.

Arm in arm, Ike and Cassie walked to the facing bench before the people of the congregation. Father and Mother Ballinger sat beside Cassie; Wesley and Rachel Evans sat by Ike, since his parents could not be there.

For five minutes there was silence. Then Ike and Cassie rose. Ike said firmly and solemnly, "In the presence of God and before these, our friends, I take thee, Cassie Ballinger, to be my wife, promising with Divine Assistance, to be unto thee a loving and faithful husband as long as we both shall live."

"In the presence of God, and before these, our friends," Cassie responded, "I take thee, Isaac Evans, to be my husband, promising with Divine Assistance, to be unto thee a loving and faithful wife as long as we both shall live."

A table was brought forward by the Friends who had seated the congregation. It held the marriage certificate, on which were already written the promises they had made to each other.

Ike signed his name, and below it Cassie signed the name she had just taken, Cassie Evans. So that neither brother should feel slighted, Ike had asked his brother Samuel to read aloud the words of the promises. This Samuel now did.

A meeting for worship then began. Cassie was touched when, all over the little meeting house, Friends rose and offered messages of love and encouragement to them. Truly this was the very best way in the world for anyone to be married. This was an act of God rather than of man and needed no minister to solemnize it.

After the meeting, Mother and Father held an infare. The wedding guests followed the family to the Ballinger home, where each of them signed the wedding certificate. Cassie folded the certificate carefully and placed it in the family Bible, which Father had given them, for safekeeping.

Sober refreshments were served, and Cassie was proud of her home and of the way her parents made the guests feel welcome. The Evans wives looked very respectfully at Cassie, though Cassie heard Priscilla whisper to Rachel that Mother Evans would find little plainness in Cassie's appearance in her grey dress. Indeed, even Cassie, when she had looked at herself in the mirror at home before the wedding, had felt that her happiness seemed to have made her red hair more blazing than ever.

When the infare was over and she and Ike drove away behind Ike's long-legged horse, Cassie felt a little sadness, but only for a moment. She knew that the home with Ike was the one she had always waited for, though before now, she had believed that no home could be dearer than the one she was leaving.

The new home seemed already hers, hers and Ike's. There she would live until she died—not perhaps in the same house, for already Ike planned someday to have a larger house, but on this same bit of earth.

Father had given them several hundred dollars—a dowry, he said. Ike had insisted that it be put in the bank and saved until some later time when they might be ready to add to the present house or build another. He would allow no man to help in the support of his new wife.

When they drew up in front of the little house, the shyness that Cassie had thought might afflict Ike, and even herself, lasted for only a moment. Ike lifted Cassie down from the wagon and set her on the ground briefly while he tied the horse. Then lifting her in his arms, he carried her through the door and into the house. He lighted the fire, which he had laid before he left home, and led her to the chair before it. Untying the strings of her new bonnet, he put it carefully on the table and tenderly removed her shawl.

Laying aside his own hat and greatcoat, Ike suddenly knelt before her and placed his head in her lap. Cassie put her hands lovingly on his head, then slipped down beside him on the bear-skin rug and buried herself in his arms. Ike held her fiercely, murmuring words he had surely not known he remembered —words from the Scriptures, from the book of the Song of Solomon.

"My love, my fair one, let me see thy countenance, let me hear thy voice; for sweet is thy voice, and thy countenance is comely. Thou art all fair, my love; there is no spot in thee."

Ike forgot all the things he had been led to believe about the carnality of the body, the evils of the flesh. This love he had for Cassie, and she for him, was as good and as beautiful as the flowers and the trees that grew around the little house.

With trembling but tender hands, his big fingers finding a new skill, he unfastened the myriad buttons of Cassie's wedding dress and learned with her the true nature of marriage.

The horse fastened to the hitching post outside was forgotten.

When Ike went out, it was dusk, and he spoke soothingly to the horse, which had waited so patiently. Then he took in the big chest filled with Cassie's belongings and left to care for the horse.

Cassie looked into the mirror and saw the disorder of her red, curly hair, now all unbound around her small white face. Her eyes seemed almost green, and there was a flush in her cheeks. In the half light of the late afternoon, her dark brows and lashes looked almost black. Her lips were red, bruised by Ike's kisses.

She would put on the green dressing gown that Father had brought her long ago from Philadelphia. She had kept it in her chest all this while. They would eat the supper that Mother had packed in a basket, and she would wear the green gown. Ike would think the gown worldly, perhaps, but he would think it lovely, too.

Cassie picked up her dress and petticoats from the chair where Ike had put them as he removed them one by one. So comfortable had she been in his arms that Cassie felt as completely a part of Ike as if they had been married for fifty years.

As she opened the cupboard, she saw the lovely dishes that Father had ordered from the East for her. Tonight they would use only their best. She took out the silver spoons and placed them beside the bone-handled knives and forks. Then she opened the basket. Inside were sliced ham on a milk-glass plate, eggs pickled in beet juice, one of Mother's best mince pies, and pickled peaches in a green glass jar. Cassie placed a white linen cloth on the drop-leaf table and spread the food on it.

Ike came to the door, and Cassie met him there in her green gown. "Thee looks like a little creature of the forest in thy green gown—a beautiful little bird!" he said shyly. He was self-conscious now, a little embarrassed, perhaps, at his surrender to his instinct.

For a moment Cassie was hurt that he seemed to have escaped so quickly from his feeling of the hour before. Then, understanding so well his nature, she followed him to the bedroom, where he placed the chest, and held him close, saying, "Ike, Ike, thee is a wonderful husband."

"Cassie," he said in confusion, "I had not thought to take thee without thought and respect. Will thee forgive me?"

"Ike, it would be hard to forgive thee had thee taken me otherwise. Love is not a thing for thinking, but for feeling. Does thee not know that, my dearest?"

"Thee is right, Cassie. I do see what thee means. Thee will teach me to be free and happy, and properly loving."

"Yes, Ike, but thee will not need to be taught, only to follow the moving of thy loving spirit. Thee knows all the things thee needs to know—in thy spirit."

"I did not know that I would find these things so right and so good. Paul has said—"

"Let us not know what Paul has said. Let us think of Solomon, of Ruth and Boaz. Paul was not speaking of the kind of love we have for each other.

"Ike, thee had better not ever think that thee married me only because thee felt it was better to marry than to burn! I will not be thy choice between two evils!"

Ike suddenly gave a great shout of laughter and, picking Cassie up in his big hands, swung her wildly around the room. "Cassie, Cassie, thee an evil! Thee is so little and so clever. Thee will be a wellspring of joy to my house. That I can see!"

Cassie thought with joyful thanksgiving that already Ike had begun to see that life could be gay. Marriage had already changed him, had made him the man she had hoped to find. If Father could hear him, he would be surprised.

And Cassie laughed with Ike, though her laughter was at the picture of surprise on Father's face if he could see Ike now.

Cassie went back to the table and finished her preparations for supper, while Ike changed into his work clothes and did the evening chores. When he had finished, Ike came back in and dressed again in his wedding clothes.

"Thee is a very handsome man, Ike," Cassie said. "Will thee come and eat supper with me?"

They sat across the table from each other, the white cloth between them, with the food almost as brightly colored as Cassie's hair and dress. Ike looked at her with such love that Cassie felt a warm, melting sensation all through her. Could anything be more right than this? Even Father must agree if he could see the look in Ike's eyes.

They bowed their heads in silent thanks, and suddenly Ike was moved to raise his voice to God. "Dear Father, we thank

Thee for the gifts of Thy bounty. Help us to do Thy will, and always witness Thy truth. Bless this home, and help us to live in it according to Thy will. Amen."

Cassie added her prayer. "Dear God, help us also to keep the joy of our love. Amen."

"Joy means a great deal to thee, Cassie," said Ike thoughtfully.

"Yes, Ike, we were meant to be joyful."

"But what if there is sorrow, and times are hard for us—does thee think we can be joyful then?"

"If we are joyful, things will not be so hard for us. Does thee not see that, Ike? Sometimes it seems to me that the people who expect sorrow are the ones to whom it comes. Almost as though, in so much thinking of it, they bring it upon themselves. Let us expect the best. Then if bad comes, we will not already have sorrowed for it, and so sorrow twice."

"With thee, Cassie, a man must be joyful. Thee is truly the delight of my life."

"Thee must tell me that often, Ike. Then I will continue to be."

Cassie had thought her happiness so great it could be no greater. But as she wakened each morning and found Ike beside her, as she saw him across the table at mealtimes, life became daily a better thing.

When Father came to see them, he said, "Thee must be very happy, Cassie; thee has a shining light on thy face."

Cassie answered gravely, "My whole life has been full of happiness. First with thee and with Mother, and now with Ike. But it was thee who taught me to be happy, that it is good to be gay."

Father laughed. "Thy whole life is only seventeen years.

There is much before thee, Cassie. Life cannot be all happiness. There will be sorrow, but with God's help thee will know how to handle that too. Of that I am assured."

"Thee sees that Ike is happier too, that the solemn look thee did not like is almost gone from his face?"

"Yes, that is true. But it would be sad indeed if a man were not happy when first he has the wife he wishes. Wait until thee begins to quarrel with him and see. Thee is not always sweet. Thee can be very impatient when thee finds things going wrong for thee. And, no doubt, they will go wrong at times. Thee will be tired at thy unaccustomed tasks. No doubt thy work will wear thee out sometimes, and thee will take thy tiredness out on Ike."

"Father, thee is teasing. How could I ever be impatient with Ike?"

"We will see, Cassie. We will see. But thee will come out all right in the end."

⤙ XI ⤚

THIS MORNING CASSIE WAKENED WITH THE SENSE THAT SOME-thing special was about to happen. To her, every new day was undiscovered country. But in all the eight months of her married life, as she had learned to sew, cook, and keep house, there had been a lurking sense of foreboding, which she could never completely put out of her mind. At last the dreaded time was upon her.

Today they would take the train from Greenbury and go to see Mother and Father Evans. Was just the order of their names in her mind an indication of their natures? In thinking of her own parents, it was always Father and Mother Ballinger, as Mother would have it be.

Cassie would soon know if she could win approval in Ike's mother's eyes. She did not feel this dread about Father Evans. It was only the things Ike had said about his mother without knowing he said them that worried Cassie. She would not have a dog in the house. How would she feel if she knew that Nick slept each night beside their fire?

Now Cassie knew where the saying "Idle words! Idle words!" so often used by Samuel and Wesley was learned. Even Ike at times seemed to feel that Father's humorous speeches were "idle words." Sometimes, when Cassie spoke lightly, she could almost see the saying form on Ike's lips. Or did she only imagine this when she felt guilty for saying things that shocked Ike? She could not be sure.

Cassie pulled the comforter up around her neck and tried to enjoy a few minutes more of the warmth and pleasantness of staying in bed when she knew she should be getting up. But alas, this day was too momentous.

She reached over and placed her hand on Ike's big shoulder and shook it a little. "Ike, it is morning. Thee must get up and milk the cow."

Ike stirred and shook off her hand. But she knew that only his sleepiness could cause such an action. When he wakened he would not be cross.

"Ike, wake up. Does thee not remember what day this is? Today we go to see thy parents."

Cassie thought that a shadow crossed Ike's sleepy face, that he closed his eyes more tightly, as if to ward off the knowledge that must come with the waking day. Was there on his face some of the dread she herself felt? Surely there should be only joy in seeing one's parents after so long.

The bag was packed ready for the journey. Enos Elliott was to milk the cow, attend to the chickens, and feed Nick while they were gone. They would stay a week, or that was their present plan.

Cassie did not wish to decide finally until they had reached Ike's home and she had seen what kind of welcome they might receive. She scarcely admitted this to herself, though she seldom deceived herself in anything. Ike seemed to sense her wish, or else he agreed with her, so no definite date had been set for their return.

Now with one accord they climbed from the bed and hurried in before the fireplace. Ike had kindling ready, and quickly the warmth of the fire gave some comfort as Cassie climbed into her clothes. The underwear was cold, and the stays were like ice, even through the layers of underclothing. But by the time her shoes were laced, the room was warmer, and she prepared a quick breakfast while Ike did the chores.

They were on their way to Greenbury by six-thirty, for they must catch the ten-o'clock train and the drive was long. If only Cassie did not have this dread of meeting Mother Evans, she could enjoy the trip. Riding the train would be a pleasure in itself.

She was proud of Ike in his heavy coat and the beaver hat she had bought for his birthday, with money she had earned teaching school. This Ike could not resent. He had gazed at her gift with pride and thankfulness—with only a little mixture of doubt. "But, Cassie," he had said, "thee should have kept the money to buy thee a new dress at some time when we are short of money. Thee should not spend it for me."

But now, as they left the horse and wagon in a livery stable and walked down the stone streets to the railroad station, Cassie was happy that she had bought the hat. Ike looked as she liked to see him. In the heavy coat and the fine hat, he might feel

73

more free to be the new Ike he had become since leaving his mother's home.

Even Father could have found nothing to criticize in Ike's appearance. And Father was very particular about his own clothing—only the best material pleased him. It must, of course, be plain; but fine material was necessary for Father's sense of well-being. Cassie, too, had some of this feeling though not as much as Father.

Cassie wore the wedding dress. With the lovely bonnet and shawl, she believed that Ike's mother could not say that she was not a credit to Ike. Or would Mother Evans think instead that Cassie was vain, not a proper wife for her son? Cassie shivered a little in the crisp weather of this Eleventh Month.

The train trip was pure joy for Cassie. Ike had ridden on the train more than she, for trains were usual near his home. He was attentive to her comfort, even brushing the seat carefully before he allowed her to sit. Cassie felt really a woman grown as she looked over the other passengers on the train.

It was late in the evening when they arrived at Ike's home-town. His parents lived three miles out in the country, and Father Evans was to meet them at the station.

When Cassie saw an old gentleman with a long white beard, she somehow knew that this was Father Evans. It was not that he was so much like Ike, for Ike had already told her that he looked like his mother's people. It was perhaps the kindness in his blue eyes, the smile, which was Ike's when he was most joyful, that told her.

Ike said proudly, "Father, this is thy new daughter, Cassie."

Father Evans bent down only a little, for he was not as tall as Ike, and kissed Cassie's cheek. His lips were cool and dry under the white beard.

"Thee has chosen well, Ike; that is clear. We are glad to have thee for a daughter, Cassie."

Would *we* be correct? Cassie wondered. Could Father Evans speak for his wife? Would she echo his words? Cassie, who had never found cause to be afraid of anyone, was afraid now. If she did not love Ike so much, or if she did not see that Ike truly loved his mother greatly, she would not be so concerned.

Cassie said warmly, "Thee looks as thee should look to be Ike's father. I knew thee must be the one when I first saw thee waiting there."

"Did thee? Ike's mother always says that Ike looks like her people."

"He has thy smile, Father."

Ike added, with a tone that made Cassie look quickly into his face, "It is smiles that Cassie sees."

Cassie said reproachfully, "Ike, thy father will think thy wife light-minded."

Ike's smile was tender, but the look of dread was now on his face and not just in Cassie's mind.

"Thee knows I would not mean that, Cassie. But thee does not approve of soberness, thee knows."

Father Evans gave Cassie a look of great understanding. Suddenly a new thought came to her: all married people, or at least many of them, were divided into opposites. Her own father was forward-thinking and gay; her mother was more like the other Friends, who were not so gay as Father Ballinger. Father Evans was kind, had a gentle sort of humor, and wanted things to be pleasant and happy, even as Cassie did. Mother Evans would be firm and stern, unyielding in her knowledge of what was right and proper. Was Ike's mother the kind of person that Father would call not righteous, but self-righteous?

Cassie, too, would be firm. Mother Evans would not frighten her, nor would she put her in the wrong with Ike. Yet it seemed to Cassie that, as they drew nearer to the Evans homestead, Ike's expression changed, and his long upper lip seemed to set more uncompromisingly against his lower one. Mother Evans would be ready to change Ike back into the sober young man who had been so disapproving on that First Day morning when Cassie almost smiled at him over the partition.

With quick resolution, Cassie lifted her chin. Mother Evans would not make Ike unhappy—nor her, either. She would see to that. She, too, had changed from the young girl who had fallen in love with Ike only a little over a year ago. Marriage to someone like Ike, who was so kind and good that at times it made her feel guilty and unworthy just to be loved by him, made her older, more able to cope with life and the people who would do harm to those she loved.

Cassie would find out when she saw Mother Evans if she was not good for Ike. If she was not, they would go home without finishing their visit. Cassie was not the daughter of William and Faith Ballinger for nothing!

Ike put a protecting arm around Cassie and helped her from his father's light wagon. But as they came close to the door, his arm seemed to stiffen and become uncomfortable, as though he wished somehow it were not there, as though it did not belong to him, so strange it felt. Yet he kept it there as if he feared Cassie would need its strength.

But Cassie needed no protection now; she had God's help in this matter. And if Mother Evans thought that her God was a different one from Cassie's, Cassie knew by the witness of the Spirit that hers was the One and the only One, regardless of the mistaken ideas of the self-righteous.

She smiled up into Ike's face to tell him that she loved him with her whole heart, that together they need fear nothing, not even the disapproval of those who were too sure of their rightness. As she smiled, she slipped out of the circle of his arm and knew that Ike was relieved.

Never, never, never would she make her children feel this sense of guilt because of fear of her disapproval! Cassie would wish her own children to feel the guiding of conscience, but this was not conscience; this was Mother Evans's intolerance.

Cassie did not feel ashamed of judging Ike's mother even before she had seen her. Ike's response to the nearness of her physical presence had told her as much about his mother as the whole visit would.

The door opened, and Mother Evans stood in the entrance. She was tall—as tall for a woman as Ike was for a man. The long upper lip that, in Ike, spoke of firmness and decision, had, in Mother Evans, a downward slant at the corners. There were lines of disapproval etched around the eyes. For a moment, Cassie thought that his mother would not speak at all, but would wait until Ike forced her to. At last Mother Evans said with a difficult smile in Ike's direction, "Ike, thee is welcome."

"Mother, this is Cassie." Cassie heard Ike swallow and then say firmly, "I have brought thee a daughter."

Mother Evans leaned toward her, and it was all that Cassie could do to keep herself from pulling away as the cold dry lips touched her face. They did not touch her lips; for that Cassie thanked God. She could not have borne the cold touch on her mouth.

Mother Evans surveyed Cassie, and there was disapproval in her voice. "Thee is very young, Cassie. Thee looks delicate. Is thee sure thee is strong, strong enough for the wife of a pioneer?"

"Yes, Mother Evans. I am very strong."

It seemed to Cassie that Mother Evans was about to reach out and feel the firmness of her flesh to see if she had good muscle for hard work. It was as if she were about to be offered in a horse trade. Father was a good man in a horse trade, could tell a horse's age by its teeth. Mother Evans's eyes had the same speculative glint that Father's eyes had when he looked into a horse's mouth.

Cassie smiled widely. "My teeth, too, are sound, as thee can judge." With a small, white finger, Cassie pushed up her lip on either side, showing the pearllike teeth Ike found so beautiful.

Mother Evans's eyes blazed. It was one thing for her to insult Ike's wife. Apparently it was quite another for Ike's wife to answer back.

Full of anger toward Mother Evans, Cassie turned to Ike. Would it have made a difference in the relationship between her and her mother-in-law if she had not allowed her humor to get the upper hand? Cassie would never know, but she could never forget the hurt she saw in Ike's eyes at the unforgivable thing she had done. She had betrayed him! It was not the Spirit that had moved her to say what she had—not the Spirit of the Lord, at any rate. Poor Ike, who must have dreaded this meeting from the time he first knew that he loved her; she had truly betrayed him!

Now Cassie turned quickly, and with all her love for Ike in her voice, she said contritely, "Mother Evans, I am ashamed. I did not mean what I said as it sounded. Thee sees, my father sometimes trades in horses, and he insists that they be strong. And then he looks at their teeth. I could only think of this and said what came into my mind without thinking how it would sound to thee!"

Cassie felt that the smile on Mother Evans's face was triumphant as she replied almost graciously, "Thee is forgiven, Cassie. It is right to forgive people who do wrong. When they admit their guilt."

Cassie could barely keep from saying, *Wrong—guilt—it is not so bad as that!* But she bit back the words. If it gave Mother Evans such pleasure to put her in the wrong, and if it would make Ike feel better, she would bear it. She could even bear something that seemed like disloyalty in Ike's failing to defend her against his mother. One could understand how a man might be under the influence of his mother, if he loved his own parents as Cassie loved hers.

She was almost afraid to look at Ike. She felt alone, as if only Ike's father were truly on her side. Quickly her eyes darted to Father Evans's face. Was that a smile of amusement she saw there?

Then Ike spoke quickly, for the Spirit had moved him. "No, Mother, thee must not say that Cassie did wrong. She did perhaps speak unadvisedly, but not with guilt. Cassie is quick in everything, and sometimes speaks before she thinks. But not in any really wrong way. And thee did not have love in thy voice when thee questioned her."

Ike had not deserted her. Again she felt warmed and secure in his love. But she knew that now her situation was worse with his mother, for Ike's defense of her words would be doubly hard for Mother Evans to forgive.

"Where shall I put our bag, Mother?" There was a firmness in Ike's voice that Cassie was glad to hear, as though he were telling his mother that they would say no more of this.

Mother Evans's voice was almost sullen. "There is a fire in the front bedroom. You may take it in there, Ike." Cassie heard the *you* with a little shock. Never had Cassie's own mother called her by anything but the loving *thee* of the plain speech, even when she had found it necessary to reprimand Cassie. Truly Ike was being punished for her words—and his.

In spite of the warmth of the fire roaring in the big fireplace, Cassie felt that the very room was cold, so neatly, so exactly, was each piece of furniture placed in the room. Not one thing gave evidence that people had lived and loved in this room. Surely no one had been born or conceived in that bed. Cassie

79

shivered a little. There must have been generations of Evanses who had died there.

Ike stood looking down at her, then turned and closed the heavy door between the kitchen and the bedroom. "Cassie." His voice was low and hurt.

Before he could finish what he would say, Cassie threw herself against his chest and pressed her face into the front of his Sabbath Day coat. She could smell the harsh odor of the black wool. "Ike, does thee forgive me for what I said to thy mother? She should not speak to me as though I were a stranger thee had brought home to her. Thee knows there was no kindness in her manner."

"Thee is right, Cassie. But thee would have been wiser not to speak as thee did. My mother has forgiven thee; thee heard her say it. But it will be hard for her to forget that thee offended her with thy first words."

"She offended me with her first words. Thee saw that, too. But for thy sake I am sorry, truly sorry. I will be careful with thy mother, Ike. I promise thee."

"Thank thee, Cassie." His voice was sober, not as it had been this last year, but as when Cassie had first known him. This was what she had feared constantly as they planned their visit. But she had not thought that it would be words of hers that would bring back his mournful look.

"We must go back to Mother. She will wonder why we do not come in to the family."

Again Cassie could not help saying the thing she thought. "Thy father will not wonder. Does thee think thy mother would not know that thee is only a little while married, that thee would like to be alone with thy wife after thy trip?"

Ike's voice was completely without humor. "My mother does not approve of carnal desires."

With sudden resentment, Cassie pulled away from Ike. "Is

80

thy desire for me carnal now, Ike? Is that what thee would say?"

"No, no, Cassie, thee knows that is not what I meant. Now thee is putting a meaning in my words that is not there."

Ike stepped quickly to the door and turned the little catch that locked it, then pulled Cassie down beside him on the big four-poster bed.

"Cassie, thee must listen to me. Thee knows that the love I have for thee is not carnal, but God-given; that nothing my mother says can make me feel that it is. But thee should see, too, Cassie, that to my mother there *is* something carnal about physical love. Thee can see that my mother does not believe, as we do, that love can be good and God-given. Would thee spoil our visit with contentiousness to prove thyself right?"

Now Cassie saw that there were two sides to this: not her side and Mother Evans's, but her side and Ike's. If they loved each other, there should be only one side, and that *their* side.

"I will be good, Ike. Let us go back in to thy mother."

There was no more unpleasantness that day. Cassie listened while Ike's mother told the news of the neighborhood, listened until she could no longer keep from yawning.

She spoke admiringly of the food that Mother Evans had prepared: the pumpkin pies, the chicken and dumplings, the turnips and sweet potatoes from the cellar, where they had been kept so carefully from freezing. She admired the tatted lace of the scarf on the stand table in the big kitchen. She asked for the receipt for the cookies in the stone jar and copied it carefully to paste in the book she kept at home.

Mother Evans's cold eyes warmed a little, and Cassie told herself that it was better to be more admiring than one perhaps felt, if it would make Ike happy. If the pumpkin pie had more spice than her own mother used—and than she herself liked— everyone had the right to his own taste.

After the dishes were washed, they sat down beside the big

fireplace in the kitchen. Mother Evans turned her full attention to Cassie, but Cassie thought there was something wary in her approach, as though she had not forgotten that Cassie would not take insults without answering for herself.

"Does thee do much sewing, Cassie?"

"I am better at embroidery than plain sewing, but I am learning to make Ike's shirts now. My mother is teaching me, and she says, though I am slow, she thinks I will learn."

Mother Evans's tone was dry. "Thee will find more use for plain than fancy sewing as the wife of a farmer."

"Thee is right. Poor Ike, he will have to wear some very plain shirts before I have learned, no doubt."

Ike's smile was tender. "She does very well, Mother. Thee must not think her slow. Thee sees, she has spent many hours with her books so that she could teach the school."

This was not quite true, though Ike did not know it. Father had not thought that she would teach the school. He had only wished that she learn to use her mind, to use her mind to sharpen his own. Since Father admired Lucretia Mott and her work for women's rights, he felt that his daughter should not be limited in what she might learn.

It would be foolish to try to explain this to Ike's mother. Cassie smiled to herself as she thought how like oil and water would be a meeting between her father and Mother Evans.

The warmth after the cold journey and the early hour at which they had risen conspired to make Cassie very sleepy. Twice she found herself nodding, her head falling toward Ike's shoulder as they sat together on the daybed beside the fire.

At last Mother Evans said, her voice a little kinder, "Thee can go to bed whenever thee is ready, Cassie. Thy bed is made."

"Thank thee, Mother Evans. It has been a long day, and I did not go to sleep quickly last night, I so anticipated this visit." As Ike rose to go with her, Cassie said, "Thee need not come,

Ike. Thee must have many things to say to thy father and mother. Come when thee is ready."

It was queer that Cassie really meant a thing like that, and yet felt a little hurt when Ike took her at her word.

The bed was wide, and in spite of the fire in the room, the sheets felt cold as Cassie slid between them. She had become used to going to bed with her husband, and it was not easy to fall asleep without knowing that he was on the other side of the bed. At first Cassie had thought she could not sleep with anyone, having for so long slept alone. Now it was hard to sleep without Ike.

At last she fell asleep and did not waken until she heard Ike slipping from the bed and smelled the ham frying for breakfast. She sat up quickly.

"Good morning to thee, Cassie. Thee is a sleepyhead."

Cassie dressed quickly in the cold room. She combed her red curls and coiled the heavy braids around her small head. The grey calico dress she wore made her feel a little more at home, a little less a visitor.

"Thee looks very nice this morning, Cassie."

"Thank thee, Ike, but thee knows that 'pretty is as pretty does,' and I haven't done very pretty, I fear."

Ike kissed her gently on the top of her head and opened the door into the kitchen. Mother Evans took a great pan of brown biscuits from the oven and said, "Good morning to thee, Ike, and to thee, Cassie."

"Good morning, Mother Evans. The breakfast smells good. Can I help thee?"

"Everything is ready when Ike's father gets in from the milking."

Now the door opened, and Father Evans's bearded face appeared. His voice was warm and welcoming. "Good morning, my children. Did thee sleep well, Cassie?"

"Oh, yes. I did not hear anything until Ike got up just now. The bed was so good and so warm."

Mother Evans was a little mollified at Cassie's admiration of her bed. Perhaps she had dreaded what Cassie might think of her and her home. No doubt Priscilla and Rachel had written and told her that Cassie's home was large and Cassie's father well-to-do.

Cassie must try to think of how things would seem to Ike's mother. She would try! But it was hard to imagine Mother Evans being doubtful as to how Cassie would like her or her home.

Father Evans was husking corn, and Ike borrowed some of his father's clothes, though they were small for him, and went out into the crisp November air to help. Cassie saw him go with dread, wondering if, alone, she could cope with the questions Mother Evans would ask without again saying things she should not say.

She helped with the dishes and the making of the beds, admiring the beautiful quilts that Mother Evans had made, asking for the pattern for the one she most admired. Then, though she offered to help with the making of the pies, Mother Evans told her she would need no more help. Cassie longed to ask if she might go and watch Ike and Father Evans at their task, but knew without asking that this was not the thing she should do.

Now Mother Evans's faintly querulous voice came to her. "Is Ballinger a Scotch name, Cassie? I know no Ballinger in this neighborhood."

"No, it is French, once called de la Boulanger. My ancestor was a Huguenot who fled the persecution in France and went to England, there to become a follower of George Fox."

"French? Thee is French?"

There was no mistaking the disapproval on the stern face be-

84

fore her. It seemed that there was nothing about Cassie of which Ike's mother could approve.

"Only a little, I am afraid. Thee sees that there is only one part French to many parts English and Scotch. But my father is very proud of his French ancestry."

"The French are a frivolous people." Mother Evans spoke with authority. "It surprises me that thy father should favor that strain in his ancestry."

"My father is doubtless proud of all his ancestors, though he holds that no man is responsible for his birth. There is, however, a painting of this ancestor, and my father resembles him greatly. It is from this one that we inherit our red hair."

"It is too bad that thee could not have got the color of thy hair from one of thy other ancestors. Thy hair is very bright. Did thee never think thee should cover it with a cap to hide it?"

Cassie did not answer immediately. Father had once told her to count to ten before saying something that perhaps she should not. Now she counted with all her might.

"Thee thinks my hair is better hid?"

"It does seem very bright to me; it does not encourage plainness or simplicity."

Cassie thought that this was surely true and right. With this thought, she was able to find a smile and to answer without impertinence. "I do not think God would disapprove of the hair He has given me. My parents do not find it displeasing, nor does Ike. So I think I shall not wear a cap."

Mother Evans said no more, but Cassie could almost see the thoughts that were in her mind.

Well, she would not tell Ike that his mother thought her hair immodest, not fitting for a Friend to wear. She would not lessen Ike's joy in seeing the red of her hair against the green of the robe she wore when they were alone. Ike had had so few pleasures. His mother's disapproval had too often deprived him of a joy in beauty.

Carefully Cassie bore with Ike's mother until the men came for the noonday meal, then as carefully through the remainder of the day.

That evening some of the Friends came to see Ike and to view the wife he had taken. There was an air of surprise as they saw her, and Cassie knew that, like Father Ballinger, they would not have expected Ike to have much in common with one like Cassie. But they were friendly and clever, and Cassie enjoyed the evening.

There was one young woman to whom Mother Evans was unusually cordial, a girl who looked at Cassie with dislike in her eyes and had little to say. This girl went into the kitchen with Mother Evans to bring out the bowls of apples and popcorn as though she felt at home in the house—more at home than Cassie would ever feel. Yet Cassie experienced a pang of sympathy for this girl, who would have pleased Mother Evans as a wife for Ike, while Cassie could not. If Ike had stayed at home, perhaps he would now be married to Prudence Draper, instead of to Cassie. Cassie looked across the room to where Ike sat among the young men and gave him a little smile of love and happiness.

How sober this girl was! How sober would have been the home they made.

Cassie restrained an impulse to go to Ike and sit beside him, to feel the comforting pressure of his shoulder near hers. But that must wait until they were alone. How glad she would be when they were again in the small house across from the school! But Cassie must not hurry Ike; she must not let him know how little joy she found in this visit to his parents.

When four days were gone, it was Ike who said, "Cassie, does thee think we could go home now? Thee knows I like to visit my mother and father, but it will be nice to be at home again."

86

"Yes, Ike, I am ready when thee is. No doubt there will be much work waiting for thee when we get home."

Cassie sighed with great relief that she had gotten through these days, had not quarreled with Mother Evans after the first day. They could leave in peace and harmony.

⌐XII⌐

IT WAS GOOD TO BE HOME. IKE FINISHED PUTTING AWAY THE crops and had more time to spend in the house doing chores that he wished to have done before spring work began. Nick, no longer a pup, divided his time between Ike and Cassie, unable to decide whom he loved most.

Christmas came, and they spent the day with Father and Mother Ballinger. Ike's brother had invited them to come for the holiday dinner, and Ike had answered for Cassie: "Thank thee, Samuel, but it seems that Cassie's parents would feel too much alone this year without her. It seems better that we go there this time." Cassie had felt a great surge of love for Ike in sparing her the making of this refusal.

For Christmas gifts, Father had been determined to give Cassie and Ike some of the things they could not afford to buy for themselves. At Mother's insistence, he had stopped by one morning to ask Cassie's permission.

Cassie had answered him gently, "Father, thee knows thee must not hurt Ike's pride with thy bounty." But then she added, "But, if thee will, thee may give us a set of the works of William Shakespeare."

Father smiled at her. "Thee does not think his works pernicious, Cassie?"

"No, Father," Cassie answered gaily. "I thought thee explained thy thinking very well to the committee."

Father kissed her good-by, and as she watched him drive away, she wondered whether Ike would agree with Father or the committee.

Friends John Overman, Nathan Nicholson, and James Parrish had come one summer evening when Father was reading aloud from one of Shakespeare's tragedies.

James Parrish pointed to the leather-bound book which now lay beside Father's spectacles on the small table. "William Ballinger, does thee believe it is fitting to read such works as these to thy daughter and thy wife? They are worldly books dealing with vain and worldly things."

Father looked at him steadily and asked, "Has thee read these works thee condemns?"

James Parrish, his manner uncomfortable, said, "No, but I have been told—"

Father interrupted, "It is not right to accept hearsay as truth! Until thee has personal knowledge, thee has no right to speak." Father continued quickly, "Thee knows that George Fox has said, 'It is not the Scriptures by which man should try all doctrines, religions, and opinions, but the Holy Spirit by which the holy men of God gave forth the Scriptures.' "

James Parrish did not think as quickly as Father, so had no answer ready.

Father began to question him. "Tell me, James Parrish, from which book comes this saying, 'Be not faithless, but believing.'? Or this, 'Love sought is good, but given unsought is better.' Or this, 'Thou art beside thyself; much learning doth make thee mad.' Or this, 'They were as fed horses in the morning; everyone neighed after his neighbor's wife.' Or this, 'How sharper than a serpent's tooth it is to have a thankless child.' Does this come from Job, 'I am bound upon a wheel of fire that mine own tears do scald like molten lead'? And this, 'Men must endure their going hence, even as their coming hither.' "

"Does thee know?" Father asked as James Parrish hesitated. "Three come from the Scriptures; all the rest from the works of William Shakespeare. Does thee think the Holy Spirit did not guide this man? No ordinary man could know humanity so well as this great man who speaks from inspiration. Until thee can choose between these sayings, do not tell me I should not read such things."

After the committee had gone, Father said, "Surely the Holy Spirit led me in my answers. I had not thought to speak so. The words came to me as revelation."

"So long as thee does not mistake thy spirit of pride for the Holy Spirit," Mother answered.

Father put his hand on Mother's and said, "Thee is right, Faith. I am prone to speak too quickly, but this time thee may be assured it was the Holy Spirit."

Christmas was a very good day. Father's gift to them was his own set of Shakespeare's works.

Ike and Father found many things to discuss. Yet Cassie sensed that Ike felt a little left out when Father turned to her with some joking remark, knowing that she would understand and appreciate the fine shade of his meaning. At such times, Mother assumed an almost protective air with her son-in-law. Cassie began to understand, as she had not before, that sometimes Mother must have felt left out of the joking between her and Father.

She saw, too, that Mother enjoyed having a son. It seemed that Ike found in Mother Ballinger something he had missed in his own mother. That something was an uncritical kind of love.

With the New Year, there was little that could be done out

of doors, and Cassie encouraged Ike to read Shakespeare and the books that she had brought from home, books she had read and loved.

He would try to read with her, but she sometimes thought that he felt guilty at this "waste of time." His mother would certainly feel that way about it. There were quilts to be made, knitting that would need to be done before another winter, when perhaps she would have other responsibilities, less time.

But when Ike could overcome this feeling, she could see that he enjoyed the reading, that he got a deeper meaning from the things he read than Cassie herself did. Often, when Father was there, they discussed the books they had read, and Cassie felt a great pride in Ike's thoughtfulness and insight.

Sometimes there were differences of opinion, and sometimes it was Father who admitted that he had been mistaken. Then Cassie would smile at Father, and he would return the smile, not at all sorry to have lost, since it meant that Cassie had done well in her husband.

March came, and with it Cassie's knowledge that their time alone would be over with the coming of autumn, that a child would arrive to share their happiness. She was glad, yet a little sorry that this time of freedom would be gone. She and Ike had known each other such a short while, and each had so much to learn of the depths of character in the other.

A few days later, as they sat before the fireplace after the supper dishes had been washed and put away, Cassie said, "Ike, would thee like to be a father?"

Ike looked up quickly from the paper he was reading. "Cassie, thee means—?"

"Yes, Ike, thee will be a father in the fall."

Ike rose and came to kneel on the floor at her feet, as he did only when he felt nearest to her. He put his face in her lap and said softly, "Cassie, thee will be a good mother, so gay, so tender. I will try to take good care of thee and of our child."

"Yes, Ike, I know thee will."

Then, with a keen glance into her eyes, Ike said, "Thee is glad, Cassie? Thee is ready to leave thy girlhood, to be a mother?"

Cassie smiled. "Thee thinks I must leave my girlhood, must be old to be a mother? Did thee never think it might be nice to have a young mother, someone who was a little bit of a child with thee? They tell me that thee learns more from thy children than from thy parents. If so, it might be good to be young for the learning."

"That might well be true, but, Cassie, thee will have much work to do. More than thee has now. And with the making of the crops, I will have but little time to help thee."

Cassie sighed. "Yes, I know I have much to learn. But if thee will keep the water carried until we can have the well thee plans sometime to dig, I will get along. Thy shirts may not always be mended, but thee will not go hungry."

Ike rose to his full height and looked down at her, so little there below him. Suddenly he stooped, picked Cassie up in his arms, and carried her over to the big chair, where he seated himself.

"I will take care of thee. Did thee think I wanted only a housekeeper? If thee never learned to do the things my mother did in her house, it would not be of any great import. Thee makes me happy just by being thyself. And thy children will call thee blessed because thee is gay and has great understanding, not because thee is a good housekeeper. That will come to thee as thee grows older. It is hard to learn understanding and to be happy when thee has not started early."

"Thee is happy now, is thee not, Ike?"

"Yes, Cassie, when thee is near. Thee must help me to be happy with our children, to show them that they are loved, that life is a wonderful gift from God, not something to be borne until we reach a better shore. Until I met thee and loved thee, Cassie, I had not known that that was really true."

"Poor Ike. Thee sees that it was meant that we should meet and marry. Thee is so good; it were a sad thing that thee should not be happy, that thee should almost think it wrong to be joyous."

"Thee is right. Together we will make our children happy and help them to know that it is good to be joyful in the Lord."

It would soon be time to set the hens and plant the garden, and Cassie knew that if the gardening was to be done, she would have to help. Ike could not afford to hire the help he needed for clearing the land, and in the spring season, his neighbors and brothers would be very busy.

Father would be willing to come and help when Cassie became too busy, for he loved gardening and would consider it a pleasure. Though the Ballingers lived on their farm, Father did not do much active work in his fields. Before he came to Indiana, he had lived for some years in Ohio, where he had added to an inheritance left him by his father. Now it was not necessary for him to do heavy labor.

If only Ike would not resent Father's help. If Ike did not know that Father paid a hand for most of his own gardening, he would not mind so much. It was queer that a man could accept help from a poor man, help which seemed like charity when the giver was well off and had time to give the assistance. But Father respected Ike's feeling in this matter, and seldom—or as seldom as he could manage—did he trespass on Ike's pride.

Mother and Father came over to spend the next First Day, and Cassie could hardly wait to break the news of the baby to them. There were families who did not discuss such things, held

92

it immodest, but the Ballingers did not have this feeling, and Ike was beginning to understand their attitude in such matters.

After dinner was over and they were seated around the fire in the big kitchen, Cassie said gaily, "Mother, would thee feel very old if thee were to be a grandmother one of these days?"

Mother did not answer, and Cassie smiled at her, for she felt sure from Mother's expression that she had guessed before a word was spoken. But Father bounded from his chair as Cassie believed the Frenchmen she had read about must bound and, taking her hand, kissed her gently on the forehead.

"That is fine, Cassie, fine. Does thee think thee could get a grandson for thy old father?"

"Thee old? Thee only wants to be told that thee is too young to be a grandfather. Thee does not want a granddaughter, one like thy own daughter? Thee was not satisfied with me, I see now."

"See that thee brings up thy daughter better than thy parents have brought thee up, to be more respectful. As for a son—"

There was no need for Father to finish. Cassie knew what a joy a son would have been to him. She had served as well as any daughter could. But a son that Father could teach to hunt and to fish, as well as to read the books he so loved—his cup would be running over when he held a grandson in his arms.

Father turned to Ike. "My children have made me very happy today. Thee, Ike, is like a son to me. Cassie has done well in choosing a husband."

Cassie could see that this display of feeling was hard for Ike to understand, though it was plain that he found it most gratifying. To Cassie it made the happiness she felt almost more than she could contain.

Soon she and her mother were busy planning the baby's clothes while Father and Ike spoke of the spring work to be done. Cassie quickly saw that it would indeed be hard for

Father to restrain himself from giving the things her little family would need. She must somehow warn him that Ike would be no less hurt, perhaps even more, because the need might be greater. They would get along without Ike's becoming offended by his father-in-law's affluence. Cassie must see to that.

The first day that the ground was ready, Ike brought out the one-horse plow and broke up the small garden plot for planting. Cassie asked reluctantly, "Ike, would thee mind if Father came over and brought some of his seeds for our planting? Thee knows that Father is a famous gardener. It makes him very happy to show this superior knowledge."

Cassie could see a muscle jump in Ike's set jaw. It was fast becoming a familiar muscle to her and told her much.

"Thee knows, Cassie, that I prefer to support my own family."

"Yes, Ike, but if it gives Father pleasure to dig in thy ground, does thee not see that it is a selfish thing to deny him this pleasure? He will like to show us the way he thinks best."

She smiled at him pleadingly. "Thee knows what pride he takes in his garden. And what a fine gardener he is. Thee might well be happy for his advice."

Put in this light, there was little that Ike could do but agree. This time, at least, Cassie felt that she must stand out against Ike. She would badly need all Father's help if they were to have food for the summer and for the winter's needs. Ike would try, but there was a limit to what one man could do.

Ike answered slowly, "In this thee is perhaps right. If thy father wishes to show us the better ways of gardening, we will be thankful."

The next week both Mother and Father came over to spend the day and to help put in the garden. As yet, carrying the baby had made little difference in Cassie's ease of movement, and she planted seeds with Mother and put out the onion sets Father had raised.

Cassie loved the feel of the warm earth in her fingers and thought ruefully that it would be good if one had only to plant and raise the garden and need not worry about sewing for the men in the family. Cassie set her teeth with determination. She would learn. Life could not all be the things she liked best to do.

Ike stopped on his way to the field to plow and said a little stiffly, "Thee is good, Father Ballinger, to leave thy own work to come and help with ours at such a busy time."

Father found the tact for which he was known among his friends. "It is easy for an old man to get away when younger hands take over. This is old men's and women's work."

As Ike left for the field, his steps were lighter, and Cassie looked up at Father with a twinkle in her eye. "Thee is not so old as all that, Father. But it was good of thee to spare Ike so."

"Having a grandchild will doubtless make an old man of me, finish the work that having a daughter like thee has begun."

Mother rose from stooping to plant the onion sets and stretched the kinks from her back. "You two can finish the planting, and I will go in and prepare the dinner, since I know what is planned."

"Thank thee, Mother. Thee knows I would rather plant than cook, doesn't thee?"

"And that thy father wishes to show off for thee his knowledge of the growing of good vegetables."

Father's bright eyes followed Mother's slender figure as she went through the gate into the yard. "Thy mother is a very wise woman, one full of the Inner Light. We are lucky to have found such good and balanced helpmeets. Now if thee had married a man like thy father, it might not have been well for thee at all. Thy Ike is indeed a young man who will go far."

Then Father showed the little smile that meant he was going

to speak in jest about something which he meant quite seriously. "That is, if he is not too stiff-necked to take a little help along the way. Thee knows, Cassie, that all we have will be thine. Why should thee choose the hardest way when thy father is so willing to help thee?"

"Would thee really like it, Father, if Ike were willing for thee to help as thee would like? Thee knows very well thee would not. Thee helped thyself, and thee would not be too ready now to approve of Ike if he allowed thee to give him that help."

"That may all be very true, Cassie, but thee knows it will be hard for me to watch when thee must do without. It would be so simple for me to make it just a little easier for thee. At least allow me to have a well dug. Thee will need it badly when thy babies are small. And Ike is always so busy at the time when that work can be done."

"We will get it sometime, never fear, Father. I will not let him forget it."

"Thee must not nag him, Cassie. Ike might allow thee to nag him when a less settled young man would not. It would be wrong for both thee and him."

"Sometimes a woman must keep after a man to get the things done that must be done. Thee knows that. Thee thyself is apt to procrastinate at times. But I will not be cruel to Ike. That thee also knows."

"It would be cruel to censure a man for not doing more than he has the time to do. Particularly a good and kind man like Ike, who would not answer thee back or perhaps chastise thee if thee needed it."

"As thee was wont to do?" Cassie answered pertly. "Father, thee is very changeable. First Ike is wrong not to let thee give me a well, and then thee thinks me wrong when I prod him to get me a well. Can thee not make up thy mind?"

"Thee is a saucy child, Cassie. Thy parents may well have spared the rod too much in thy case."

When dinner was ready, Father walked with Cassie toward the house, his arm around her expanding waist. Ike met them at the flagstone walk, and Cassie placed her free hand in his. Was ever woman so blessed with the men who loved her? And the little child growing inside her—with God's help, he would love her, too.

⤙ XIII ⤝

THE SUMMER PASSED QUICKLY, THOUGH THE HEAT MADE CASSIE most uncomfortable. She was now larger and less able to do the things she was used to doing. Her mother came often to help with the heavier tasks, and Ike did as much to help as he could. Now that autumn was here, the garden required less work.

Sometimes it seemed to Cassie that she would be more comfortable if only there could be cold drinking water. The water became warm so quickly, and though Ike did try, it was not possible for him to keep the bucket always filled. Cassie found herself being a little sulky when Ike forgot. Yet, when she thought of what Father had said to her, she was ashamed.

Father arrived one day just as Cassie was leaving to take her small water bucket the quarter-mile to the Elliotts'. She felt that she must have a cold drink, and this seemed the only way for her to get one.

Father's voice rose angrily. "Cassie, does thee mean to tell me thee was about to walk that distance in the heat for a drink? What can Ike be thinking of, to leave thee without cold water?"

"Now, Father, thee knows that the water gets warm quickly these days. It is not Ike's fault."

"Then whose fault is it? Thee should have a well. If thy husband will not dig thee one, then thy father will see that thee has one!"

"Father, thee will do nothing of the kind. Thee will not get me a well, and thee will not mention the well to Ike. If thee wishes to be welcome in Ike's house, thee will not insult him."

Father looked at Cassie in hurt astonishment. It was not unusual for her to speak quickly in impatience, but it was most unusual for her to speak in such quiet anger to her father, whom she loved so greatly.

His voice was low and ashamed. "Cassie, thee is indeed angry with me."

"Thee knows how it must be about the well. We will have one when Ike can dig it for me. Until then, it may be that I will often wish for cold water. But no harm will be done if I cannot always be given what I wish without waiting. That thee knows."

"Thee may be right, my daughter. Thee may be right."

Cassie patted Father's cheek and smiled forgivingly at him.

But the nearer the baby's time came, the harder it was for her to be without cool water.

The baby was late. Mother had counted the days for Cassie, and the doctor that Father had insisted upon agreed with Mother. Still the baby did not come on the date they had chosen. Ike tried to be close to the house in case he was needed. Father drove by every day, until Ike became a little indignant.

"Does thy father think I will not take good care of thee, will not get thee the doctor when thee needs him?"

"Now, Ike, thee must not think wrong of Father. Thee must understand that it is because Mother had some trouble when I was born and was not able to have more children. That is why Father is afraid for me, too."

"Why did thee not tell me, Cassie? I will get one of Samuel's daughters to stay with thee, to call me if I am not close to the house. Thee must know that I am as concerned as thy father for thy safety."

"But, Ike, thee knows I do not want anyone but thee to stay with me. I like being alone with thee—and the baby."

"I know, Cassie. But thee must have someone. I will go and ask Priscilla to lend me one of her daughters."

The firmness in Ike's voice showed that he had made up his mind, and even Cassie's blandishments could not change him this time. He returned later with Esther, her clothes in the back of the wagon.

Esther was fourteen and full of moods, though a little shy. Cassie was fond of her, but she had treasured this time with no one but herself and Ike.

Esther came shyly into the room. Though she was only a little more than four years younger than Cassie, they were not well acquainted. Esther was tall like her father, and even Cassie's unusual bulk did not make her feel as large as Esther.

Cassie rose on her toes to bestow a kiss of greeting on Esther's round, young cheek. "Thee is good, Esther, to come to stay with me. Ike is too concerned, or we need not have bothered thee."

"It will be no bother, Aunt Cassie. I am glad to come. Thee should not be alone. Thee is so little and so young."

Esther's cheeks reddened as she remembered that she was speaking to an aunt who, though smaller than she, was certainly not as young. Cassie's gay laugh burst into the kitchen and cleared away Esther's shyness.

"Thee is not very old thyself, Esther, but thee is too old to call me Aunt Cassie, I think, even if thee did go to my school. Just because thee is bigger than I, thee need not sound so old."

Esther was able to laugh with Cassie now, and together they went into the little room that would be Esther's until the baby came.

Cassie spoke frankly. "Does thee know, Esther, I did not wish thee to come? But now I am glad. It will be like having a sister. I have never had anyone so close to my age to be with. We will have fun together."

"Since thee says thee did not want me, I will tell thee that I did not want much to come. I was afraid thee would think me a child and treat me as thee did in school."

"Did I *mis*treat thee in school?"

"Thee was very nice to me in school, but it would not be fun to be with thy teacher all the time. Thee now seems more like a cousin than an aunt."

"That is right. If thee thinks thy mother would not like for thee to call me Cassie, thee could say Cousin Cassie when thy parents are here."

So it was that Cassie found it could be fun to have a sister. Sometimes Ike came in from the field and found them giggling like children. Once, after they had gone to bed, he told Cassie that, while it was Cassie who had not wanted Esther, it was he who was sorry to have her here; that Cassie seemed never to have time for him now. She snuggled as close to him as her size would allow and kissed the tip of his nose.

"That is what thee gets for going against my will, Ike. But soon Esther will be gone, and we will have a son to take her place and keep me away from thee. How will thee like that?"

"I will be much relieved when thee is mine again, and not so entirely thy son's."

"Thee sounds a little jealous even before thy son gets here. What will thee be when he comes?"

"A son will be a nice thing to have, but not so nice as a wife. One has but one wife, and many sons."

"What if thee should have many daughters and no sons, Ike?"

"If they were like thee, I would not complain."

"Thee seems to be very easy to please. But I think thee is not."

"What does thee mean by that?"

"I think thee does not always say when thee is not pleased with me. I think thee would like it better if I could make thee better clothes, if I should be more like the girl thy mother would have had thee marry."

Cassie felt Ike jump slightly, and she smiled in the darkness.

"Who told thee that?"

"No one told me, Ike. But I have eyes in my head. Does thee think thy wife is blind? Poor Prudence. She would have been very good in thy house, Ike. But thee needs someone like me in thy home."

"And in my arms."

Cassie kissed him gently and, turning as nearly on her side as was now possible, slept quickly and soundly. Sometimes it was not the old, like Ike's mother and her father, who could judge as to who should be married to whom. That at least must be left to the young.

The next morning when she wakened, Cassie felt a strange little twinge. She hurried Ike off to the field as soon as breakfast was over, and then sent Esther after her mother.

Cassie was surprised at her own calmness. Truth to tell, she had been a little afraid when she considered the birth of her baby. She had heard neighbor women recount many tales of difficult childbirth when Mother had thought her in the field with Father, but instead, she had been lying on the hall couch reading.

Then too, Mother Evans had told her at great length what a difficult time she had had when Ike was born. Perhaps she had wanted Cassie to feel that her bonds to Ike were much stronger than those of a wife. Mother Evans had even made Cassie doubt her own ability to have children. "Thee is very small in thy hips, Cassie. It will go hard with thee when thee has babies," she had said.

Yet now that it was time for the baby, Cassie was no longer afraid. After all, if Ike's mother could have twelve children, surely Cassie, who so wanted her baby, could have one.

Esther, with the wisdom of an oldest child, stopped at the Elliotts' and asked Lizzie to go down and stay with Cassie while she herself went for Cassie's mother.

Cassie was a little sorry to see Lizzie, for she had thought it would be nice if she could have her child alone. When animals or the neighboring Indians had their young, they went to themselves and wished no company. It would be good if she could do likewise. But mingled with her lack of welcome for Lizzie was a great feeling of easiness she had not had before. It was three miles to her mother's. It could well be that the baby would not wait.

Together they prepared the bed and put the sheet and pillow slip on the tiny cradle Father had made. Then they sat down beside the fire to await Mother Ballinger's coming.

Long before Esther would have had time to reach Cassie's parents' home, Mother Ballinger and Esther rode into the yard. Mother alighted quickly and came into the house.

"How did thee know, Mother, that I needed thee? Thee must have met Esther on the way."

Mother's face was serene. "Why, Cassie, thee should have known I would come."

Cassie took Mother's hands, and a kind of warmth seemed to pass between them.

Mother often knew things without being told. Cassie believed the Inner Light was always with her mother and hoped that sometime she herself might experience it in the same way. It was different from her knowledge that she and Ike were meant to marry. This was an awareness all Quakers believed to be part of their lives, but in practice very few now had. Or so it seemed to Cassie, though George Fox and John Woolman had spoken so confidently of it.

A little over an hour later, the baby had arrived. Cassie lay white and spent, waiting for Ike. Mother had sent Esther for him, and he came at a run, leaving Esther far back in the field.

Cassie heard the door slam and the sound of Ike running, yet trying to be quiet. He stood over her, his face white and frightened. Seeing her so worn and pale, he seemed suddenly to realize that having a baby was a dangerous and hard thing.

"Cassie, why did thee not let them call me? Oh, Cassie, thee should not have done this! What if thee had died, and I had not been with thee? Thy mother says thee would not let her call me."

Ike knelt beside her, and Cassie saw that his eyes were filled with tears. Though it seemed to take all the strength she had, Cassie lifted her hand and placed it upon his cheek.

"Ike, thee should know I would not die and leave thee."

There was a great commotion outside, and the door burst open to admit Father, his coat flying and his shirt mussed and dirty. Behind him came the doctor, not half so disturbed as Father. Indeed, he seemed a little indignant at having been dragged here so unceremoniously to find that everything had been done.

"Cassie, why did thee not wait for the doctor? Thee knows I wished thee to have medical care!"

The doctor smiled across the bed at Mother Ballinger. "Mistress Ballinger knows as much about a normal birth as any doctor, William. Compose yourself and do not worry your daughter."

Father looked a little ashamed of his outburst and retired into a corner in silence.

Soon everyone was gone but Mother. Cassie and Ike had decided to name their son John. Much as Cassie loved Ike, she did not think his name suitable to pass on to a son. Her father's name, William, would have pleased Cassie, but somehow she felt it would not be good to ask Ike to agree to that name. It was only a feeling, and she did not mention it to anyone.

Within three days, Cassie was up and sitting beside the fire when Ike came in from work. John was on her lap, and as she gazed into his face, she thought he should indeed have been called Ike, so like his father was he. Would she be able to give him the gaiety Ike lacked? Surely there must be some of Cassie and Father Ballinger in him. Mother brought Cassie's dinner in on a tray and handed John to Ike. He held John with an awkwardness that brought a smile to Cassie's lips.

"Ike, thee seems more at home with a puppy than with thy son. Does thee think he will break? Just hold him over thy shoulder as thee did the puppy, and he will be all right."

"If I did not know thy love for thy son, I would think thee belittles him when thee compares him to a puppy."

Cassie felt such a happiness, such a warmth of love and contentment here before the fire with the people she loved, that she could scarcely contain her joy. Paul notwithstanding, marriage was certainly a good thing, to take two people so much unlike and, because they loved each other, to give them this oneness. She had seen it with Mother and Father, and now with herself and Ike. Would John, too, find someone so unlike himself, and yet make a happy marriage with her?

Mother left at the end of three weeks, and though it was hard at first to get along without her, it was nice that they could be alone with their son. Cassie saw that there was no need to fear that Ike would be jealous of John. If anything, it was she who missed Ike's undivided attention. It was to the cradle that Ike first went when he came in from the fields.

One day Cassie said teasingly, yet with seriousness, "Does thee know, Ike, I sometimes think thee is more interested in thy son than in his mother? Thee even forgot to kiss me when thee came in this noon."

Ike turned with John in his arms and said, "That is what thee gets for neglecting me when Esther was here. It was so hard to find thee and kiss thee, since thee was always off somewhere laughing with Esther, that I almost forgot the habit I had acquired."

It took Cassie a few moments to realize that Ike, solemn Ike, was teasing her in return. Smiling at her, he placed the baby in her lap and stood with his arm around the two of them.

"John and thee and me. Does thee know, Cassie, it seems we must have been very lonesome before John came, but we were not. Yet I was always lonesome before I met thee. So thee sees there is a difference."

"That was a nice thing for thee to say, Ike. Thee seems to remember how to say nice things to thy wife, even after almost two years."

"If ever I forget to say these things to thee, Cassie, it will be because thee is entirely a part of me, and a man should not be saying such things to himself, surely."

"That is very logical of thee, Ike. But does thee not know that there is little logical about love and feeling? Just keep on saying nice things to me, for I like it."

⤙XIV⤚

CASSIE LOVED THE LONG WINTER DAYS SHE SPENT AT THE QUILTing frame before the fireplace while Ike mended harness or worked on the chair he was making for John. When he had time, they would read together, though Ike still felt a kind of guilt at taking time from what he considered more useful things.

Cassie thought the reading most useful, but there were still so many things to discuss with Ike, so many things she did not know about him, and so many of her own ideas that she wished to get his opinion about.

Cassie had done much mending for Ike, but she had not yet tried to make his pants. She had made him a shirt and had put the buttonholes on the wrong side. So bemused was Ike by his love for her that he did not tell her.

Cassie had seen nothing wrong with the shirt until one day when Samuel was eating dinner with them. He looked at Ike's shirt and laughed. "Well, Ike, I see that thee is wearing thy shirt different since thee is married. Does thee like it better buttoned that way?"

Cassie did not understand; then, as she looked at Samuel's shirt, she saw that it was different. At first it seemed funny to Cassie; then she saw that it was not at all funny to Ike. He flushed and refused to look at her.

Though it did not make Cassie angry that Samuel should laugh at her mistake, she would not have him making fun of Ike.

Cassie spoke quickly, using a word she hoped Samuel would not understand. "Ike is practicing to be ambidextrous. Does thee not think that a good thing? Then he can earn money with both hands."

Samuel forced a smile, but Cassie could see that he had not found it humorous to have his joke turned back on him.

After that, Cassie took special care to see that there was nothing amusing about Ike's clothes. She was also concerned about the patches she had been adding to his work pants. There was a place beyond which one could not patch, and now that place had been reached.

The clothes that Ike must have were hard to make by hand. The material for work pants was heavy and difficult to push the needle through. The buttonholes were especially hard for Cassie. Mother of course would help, would even make them for her. But Cassie hated to ask, partly on account of Father.

She had looked in the store at the ready-made clothes, but they were rough and inferior, made as no good housewife would make them. Cassie knew that she must learn or be ashamed and, worse, make Ike ashamed of her.

One day when Mother Ballinger was visiting, Cassie said slowly, "Mother, would thee be able to help me make a pattern for some pants for Ike? He needs them very much, and I have never made any."

A day or two later, Mother returned, and between them they made a pattern. Together they cut material, and Cassie began the sewing that very evening.

Ike said, "If thee had married a man who did not work in the fields, thee would not have to wear out thy eyes and thy fingers in making such heavy things."

Cassie raised her eyes from the dark material. "Ike, thee knows that I like to do things for thee. But I will say that there are other things that I like to do better than this. Thee will not mind if the stitches are a little uneven, will thee, Ike?"

107

"Thee knows anything thee does is all right with me!"

"Even when I put the buttons on the wrong side?"

"Well, it is a bit hard to get used to such buttoning. But it keeps the wind out just as well."

"Thee must tell me when I make mistakes, Ike. Thee knows I would not have thee held up to scorn because thee has married a woman who knows how to do so little."

"I would not trade thee for any woman, no matter how well she could make shirts and pants. Thee does the important things well, such as making a man happy and loving thy son. Thee is a fine cook, too. And what other wife knows Greek and Latin? Thee is a most unusual and excellent wife, Cassie."

"Thank thee, my husband. I will learn the other things. Thee will see."

When the pants were finished, Ike put them on slowly. Cassie knew that he had forebodings as to their fit. But Cassie and her mother had modeled them from the suit Ike had had made for his wedding, and they were much better fitting than his old everyday clothes, the ones his mother had made, and they covered him more adequately.

Ike would never know the tears she had shed over her work, the seams she had ripped out as she learned. Oh, but it was worth it when she saw the pride in his eyes. With this new accomplishment Cassie felt such a sense of achievement that never again would sewing be so hard for her.

Early one morning when John wakened and cried, Cassie brought him out of his cradle and gave him her breast. As she lay awake, she heard outside the windows the chirping of birds —far off, at first, in the deep green of the uncleared forest, then nearer and nearer as others joined in, until just outside the window it seemed like the melody of a heavenly choir.

Cassie thought wistfully that, if God did not object to the birds making such wonderful music, perhaps the Friends were wrong when they felt He would not like singing and organ music in meeting. Maybe it would make the feeling of God closer, as it was now to Cassie. She had heard these sounds before, but never had she felt so completely a part of nature and all its manifestations, a part of the swelling melody of beauty, of God. Oh, to wake Ike, to share with him this wonderful sense of being part of God!

But would Ike be able to share it so early in the morning, when he was sleepy? Father would have understood, had she wakened him, but Father could never have given her this sense of peace and serenity that she found in Ike. She had learned from Ike to be quiet, to wait for times like this. She and Father were always so busy with their talking that there were things they sometimes missed. Mother sometimes quoted the Psalm, "Be still and know that I am God." Father and Cassie did seem to talk more than other Friends.

Never had Cassie known a spring so beautiful, so rewarding. It was good to work in her garden this year. She felt knowledgeable since she had helped to make one last year. Making a garden was a little like caring for a baby. One must know some of the methods before one can feel the deep surge of joy at working in the soil.

At first Cassie had worried about caring for John, had been afraid that he might break in her hands, he felt so tiny, so fragile; but as she became more skillful, she knew that she could hold him close to her and trust her instincts in the ways she cared for him. It would surely be easier with a second baby than with the first.

Ike, too, was busy with the new season. There was land still to be cleared, new land to be broken. There seemed never enough daylight to do the things he wished. It was harder for Ike than for his brothers, who were older and had sons to help them. Ike wished to go ahead too quickly, to give her the things it had taken Father years to give Mother.

Cassie offered to help, but Ike replied, "No wife of mine shall work in the fields. Thy father would be right in thinking thee had married ill if I should allow that. It is enough that thee must do the gardening and the housework, besides caring for John. I did not marry thee for a hand in the fields."

There was again no time for digging the well. With the baby washing, Cassie wished daily for a well outside the door. When the weather was dry, the barrels under the rain spouts could not hold enough for the constant need. Ike tried hard to remember to bring water from the Elliotts', but when the push of work was greatest, he sometimes forgot. Cassie could not keep the reproach from her voice when she had to remind him.

Once Cassie was so thirsty that she feared the lack of water would cut down on her milk for John. She left John asleep while she walked to the well. To make matters worse, Father Ballinger was waiting for her when she returned. This time he said nothing, but looked the things he did not say. It was good that he did not comment, for, though she might agree with him about the well, she would brook no such criticism from him.

It was hard now for Cassie to realize that, not many seasons ago, she had been impatient with the slowness of time, had wished to rush ahead to meet life. Now there were always tasks waiting.

She was thankful for the time she must spend with John at her breast. Then she could enjoy his soft weight against her arm, could look into his solemn baby face and feel the rush of love she always had for him.

With the passing of the spring there was a little slowing of the work, time to enjoy the visits of Father and Mother, even picnics in the wood behind the cornfield. Ike had to be forced to take the time, for there was always something he could be doing.

Yet Ike entered into the little holidays and showed an aptitude for play that Cassie had not seen before. He was very good at horseshoes and could beat Father whenever he chose. She could not forbear teasing Father, who seemed unable to resist a slight air of superiority when it came to books.

Before it seemed possible, harvest time arrived, and then Christmas. And with it came the knowledge that there would be another child.

Cassie was glad, willing again to give herself to the process of nature. Yet she was reluctant to tell Ike, who felt his responsibility so strongly. She would wait for a likely time.

Only Ike, too, had learned some of the facts of nature. When she was forced to rise hastily from the breakfast table, her face pale, and hurry from the room, he asked her, "Cassie, are we to have another child?"

"Yes, Ike."

"But why did thee not tell me, Cassie? Is thee not glad, that thee should keep it from me?"

"Ike, I only feared it might concern thee, worry thee that we must so soon have another mouth to feed."

"Cassie, thee does me an injustice. It is only the thought of thy trial that gives me concern. It is the mother who might well regret the frequent babies, surely not the father. Does thee think I might be unable to provide for our family?"

"Oh, Ike, thee knows it is not that. But thee works so hard already."

"And thee does not, Cassie? I am sure thy father would not

put it so. I can see how reproachfully he looks at thy hands when thee must be always washing and doing things he had not planned for thee to do."

"Ike, thee makes me very unhappy when thee speaks so. Has thee ever had reason to think me sorry for our marriage? It does seem thee must be trying to make me dissatisfied with my lot. It would not be so hard had Father allowed Mother to teach me the many things I need to know. Thee thinks Father impractical I can see, but I could wish thee did not always remind me of it."

Ike looked at her in amazement. He had been speaking about Father Ballinger reproaching him. How had it got around to Ike reproaching Father?

Ike laughed and said, "Cassie, thee is very clever. Thee has put me in the wrong again." Kissing her tenderly, he added, "Cassie, thee could never give me too many children if thee continued to wish them. Thee has such good children if John is a sample."

"Ah, but John is like thee. The next may be like me, or like my father."

"That would be good, a little red-headed daughter like thee and, so, like thy father."

The days flowed one into another with quiet serenity. Now Cassie seemed able to do her work easily. John was a good baby, and this spring Ike seemed more willing for Father to spend time helping Cassie in her garden. Ike appeared to understand at last that this gave Father pleasure, and his near jealousy of Cassie's relationship with her father seemed to be lessening.

Sometimes Cassie saw Mother and Ike talking, almost as though there were some secret understanding between them. Ike would join Mother's understanding smile when Cassie and

Father became so interested in some project or some book that they were almost unaware of others in the room.

At Ike's insistence, Father and Mother spent an increasing amount of time with them. There was fondness in Ike's manner to Mother, which pleased Cassie greatly. It was as if he would make up to Mother for the hours with her daughter, the closeness to Cassie, which she had given up that Father might enjoy it.

Ike, also, was quick to spare Mother. When they were at the Ballingers', Ike waited on her, carried in her water, and would not allow her to lift the sticks of wood to put in the big fireplace.

Had Ike's mother exacted this kind of attention from him? Cassie did not think so. She might indeed have shown a martyred face because he did not wait on her more. But she would have done the tasks first to put Ike in the wrong.

Once, in June, when there were to be haying hands and Mother wished to help Cassie, Ike said, "Thy mother looks a little tired, Cassie. We must not impose on her." He rode over to his brother's and brought Esther back to help.

At first Cassie thought that Ike still felt his old reluctance to accept help, even that kind of help from Mother. Then it came to her that Ike felt that she had been selfish with Mother, that Mother had truly suffered at her hands, and at Father's. In his own occasional hurt, Ike had seen Mother's situation and had been doubly drawn to her.

Had it been Cassie who had seen such a fault in Ike, she might well have told him of the selfishness she saw. Instead, Ike tried to remedy the situation himself and not hurt Cassie by his opinion.

Back of her hurt that Ike should find her selfish was a new appreciation of both Mother and Ike. Cassie would be more thoughtful herself. No doubt she had become too used to being the center of Father's and Mother's world. And she had expected Ike to join them in spoiling her. It was well that she should be getting a family so quickly.

XV

WITHOUT ASKING THIS TIME, IKE ARRANGED FOR ESTHER TO COME again and stay with Cassie to spare her the hard work that someone must do.

Esther was now within a year of being as old as Cassie had been when she first loved Ike, and it seemed that, in just a few months, Esther had suddenly become a grown woman. Cassie gazed at her in surprise as Ike carried her bag into the room. Strange how one day you saw a girl, and then almost overnight, that girl had become a woman, perhaps ready for love and marriage.

What had seemed before to be almost overlargeness was now just a lovely, slender tallness. Esther was dark and quite as striking as Ike said Cassie herself was, but in an altogether different way. Cassie just stared at Esther in enjoyment and thought of the words of the Song of Solomon: "Thy lips are like a thread of scarlet, thy neck is as a tower of ivory." She had never believed that any daughter of Samuel and Priscilla could look like this!

Esther had become quieter than before, so when she did speak, Cassie and Ike both found themselves listening with interest. Cassie had wished that the little girl she hoped to have would look like herself. Now she saw that this was vain of her, not a thing that a truly modest person would hope. Any mother could well be proud of a daughter who looked even a little like this niece of Ike's, this daughter of Samuel's.

The next morning they worked together pleasantly, though it did seem to Cassie that Esther appeared to have something on her mind, some concern about which she did not speak. They gave the house a very good cleaning, for Cassie knew it would not be many weeks before the baby came, and it would be well to have everything in good shape.

After dinner they sat down to finish some sewing for the baby and to do some darning on John's and Ike's socks. Suddenly Cassie saw that Esther was not sewing, but sitting still with her hands in the midst of the socks in her lap. Her brow was furrowed and her eyes even darker than usual.

"Cassie—"

Cassie waited, her own hands busy with the tiny ruffles for the new baby.

At last Esther continued. "Cassie, did thee ever consider that thee might have married a man not in the meeting?"

Cassie kept her voice calm, feeling that, if she wished to help Esther, she must not show her surprise. "No, Esther, I had thought little of any young man until I saw Ike and knew that he was the one for me."

For a few moments Esther was silent; then she asked with excitement in her voice, "Does thee know Thomas Keith, the young man who bought the Hunt place next to ours?"

"I have heard Father speak of him often lately. And I saw him once when he came to talk to Father, but only from the yard, as he did not come in."

"Oh, Cassie, thee should see him; thee should know him! As thee says of thy love for Ike, Cassie, I knew when first I saw him that—" She hesitated; then, speaking with a defiant tone Cassie had never heard in her voice, she said, "that he had only to call and I would follow him anywhere."

"Has thee met him, Esther?"

"Yes, I went once to hunt our turkeys in the woods, and he

was there, seeking a horse that had wandered away. Cassie, he, too, knew when first he saw me that we were meant for each other. Thee can see, can thee not, that God would not give us each this knowledge and not wish for us to marry? Oh, Cassie, what shall I do? Thee knows that Father and Mother will never consent to it."

Then, with the defiance back in her manner, "But no one shall stop me, Cassie, *no one*. If they do not let me marry him, I shall go to him anyway."

Cassie said slowly, "But if he is such a man as my father says, he would not allow thee to do such a thing."

"Then I shall run away and marry him. I shall *make* him marry me! No one can keep him from me."

Cassie felt a thrill of admiration. It seemed only a little while since Esther had been a shy, biddable young girl, not at all like this striking young woman who would not be told that she could not marry the man she chose.

When Cassie had seen Thomas Keith, even though it was from a distance, she had thought that here was the kind of young man she herself had imagined she would marry—not, of course, if he had not been in the meeting, but he was the kind of man that a young girl dreams about.

Dark as Esther was dark, tall enough to make Esther feel as small as Cassie felt with Ike, Thomas Keith had nothing of the look of a farmer or a pioneer in his dress or bearing. Oh, it was not hard for Cassie to understand Esther's feeling. And now that Cassie saw Esther as she had become, she could see that Thomas Keith could well feel as Esther did.

This was trouble—trouble for Esther, for Samuel and Priscilla, and trouble for Thomas Keith.

And by bringing this problem to Cassie, Esther had drawn her and Ike in too. Cassie would not wish her own daughter to marry out of the meeting, but she knew that, if it came to choosing sides, she must of necessity be with Esther. She had come to love Esther two years ago, and now that Esther was a woman and had come to her with this, there seemed an even greater bond between them. What settling could there be of such a problem?

"Well, Cassie, what would thee advise us to do?"

Cassie let the ruffles lie in her lap and gave her full attention to Esther.

"Thee does not really wish my advice, Esther. Thee has said thy mind is made up. It seems to be up to this young man whether thee shall marry him or not. What does he say?"

Esther's face flushed angrily. "Is thee saying that thee does not believe he would wish to marry me, that thee thinks me not clever enough for Thomas?"

"Thee knows I did not say that. Or think that. Ever since thee came yesterday I have been thinking how beautiful thee is, how ready thee is for love." Cassie knew that Esther's mother and father would not like her to say such things to their daughter, that it would seem like encouraging her in her willfulness.

Esther's face flushed with a different kind of feeling, and she seemed a little more the child who had helped Cassie before. "Thank thee, Cassie. One day it seems to me that I must be as beautiful as Thomas says, and then I wonder that he could find me to his taste at all. It seems this must be a dream from which I shall waken."

"Thee need not worry about that," Cassie replied. With a little of her mother's dryness, she added, "Thee will have enough to worry about without that."

"Thee sees I need someone to advise me. Father and Mother do not even know that I *know* Thomas. When they find that we are going to marry—oh, Cassie, thee knows I have always been obedient in important things. But I cannot be in this. Father will be angry. And they will take my name from the meeting, but it will not stop me. I think this time, at least, the meeting must be wrong to have made a rule that is so unjust."

Cassie sighed. "No doubt all rules are wrong in someone's eyes. Does thee mind if I tell thy Uncle Ike about this?"

Esther hesitated, then said, "No, thee might as well. They will all know when the time comes. Maybe Uncle Ike can talk to Father. Father has great respect for him, partly, I think, because he is married to thee."

Cassie said slowly, "Not, I think, because he finds me such a suitable wife."

"Thee is probably right there. It would be because thy father has great possessions. And Father does respect the getting of riches. Too much, I sometimes think."

Cassie did not voice the agreement she felt.

After they had gone to bed that night, Cassie told Ike of her conversation with Esther, wondering what his reaction would be, what advice he would give.

"Thy father is a friend of this Keith, is he not, Cassie? It seems I have heard him speak of him."

"Yes, Ike. Though I myself have never met him there, he visits Father and Mother often."

"It seems that it would be better if some of Esther's family were to meet this young man, to find if his intentions are right toward Esther. She is just a child—" Ike hesitated, then said slowly, "No, of course she is not a child. Anyone can see that Esther is a woman grown, that she will do what she says. But it will be best for us to let this man see that she is not a girl with whom any man can trifle."

Cassie thought angrily that Ike should know that any man Father thought so admirable would not be one to trifle with a young girl. But, to be honest with herself, she knew that there were men, good in other ways, who might well be carried away by a beauty like Esther's. Ike could be right. Esther showed little indication that she would prove to this young man that she was not a girl to be trifled with.

"Does thee think it might be good to ask thy father and mother, and thy father's friend, Thomas Keith, to supper one night this week—that we may meet him and judge his character? Of course, Samuel and Priscilla could well object to this, but if Esther is so headstrong as thee says, we must take the risk."

Cassie spoke admiringly. "Ike, thee is a very wise man. It is what we should do. I foresee that there is to be trouble about this. And it will be better for us to know the man with whom we have to deal."

Ike rode over to Father's the next morning and went with him to deliver the invitation to Thomas Keith. When he returned, he waited until Esther had gone out to the garden and then said, "Cassie, thee is right; there is sure to be great trouble. Thomas Keith seems like a very worthy young man, though not of our faith, one for whom any young woman might well be willing to throw her cap over the mill."

Ike continued slowly, "I think thy father must see that this is the young man he would have liked for thee. In his forward-thinking manner, he could well have given thee his permission in spite of the disapproval of the meeting."

"Ike, what is thee talking about? Thee knows that my father is pleased with thee, that he sees now that our marriage was right and good."

"He is reconciled, that I can see. But this Thomas Keith has learning, is a man from the East, is all the things thy father wished for thee and thought thee would find."

The supper went off well. Esther sat beside Thomas at the table, which was spread as far as it would go, and her cheeks were almost as scarlet as her lips. Thomas treated her as Cassie believed a queen would expect to be treated. The conversation around the table was the kind Father liked. He himself was clever in what Cassie privately thought his most French manner.

Ike looked a little shocked when Father said gaily, "Thomas, thee must watch these Indiana Friends. Some of them would see nothing wrong in driving a sharp bargain. They might think thee must learn to look after thyself in a trade, and in little things they will be glad to help thee learn. Thee knows even a Quaker cannot be trusted in a horse trade."

Thomas said ruefully, "I know. I learned that soon after I came. The horse I rode today was not what I expected him to be when I bought him. Even the farm I purchased came higher than I would now pay, after having been here for this length of time."

Esther interrupted. "Thee does not mention that it was my own father and my uncle who sold thee thy seed at such a goodly price—for them, I mean."

Thomas smiled at her gently and said, "Do not worry about that, Esther. It was good seed."

"Yes, a Friend does usually give good measure," Father said. "But if he gets well paid for it, he does not think he has been dishonest, only careful."

Ike had nothing to say, and Cassie knew he was ashamed that his brothers had taken advantage of this young man, even before they were aware that he was about to take a daughter out of the meeting.

Mother interrupted quickly. "There are other things than money-making in this community, Thomas. Thee would have to go far to find better land, or a better-made house than the one thee has bought from the Friends. At least thee can see that Quakers like things to be well made, that they take care of the things they have. Not that I would excuse them in any way. Ike, why does thee not tell Thomas about the fish and wild animals we have in this new country?"

Ike replied, "Thomas, thee has as fine a stream in thy back pasture as can be found. When winter comes, thee will find the deer come to thy barnyard. It is a fine sight to watch them in the moonlight. If thee cares for venison, thee can easily have all thee wishes. Our little farm here is too near other houses for us to have this advantage, though it will be good when our children start to school that they need only walk across the road."

"Will you show me how best to hunt and dress the deer?" Thomas asked eagerly. "That is something we no longer see at my home in the East."

Cassie said quickly, "There is no one better able to speak about the wild animals here. And Ike is good with domestic animals too. Thee will find that he is not one of the Friends who will teach thee to watch out for thyself."

"I know that already," Thomas said with a warm smile.

Father seemed surprised that Ike should talk so much. Yet Ike's talk was interesting and well informed. Thomas Keith listened with respect as Ike spoke of the methods he was using in his farming. About them, Keith knew little and wished to learn.

When the guests were gone, Esther turned eagerly to Ike and Cassie. "What do you think of Thomas? You see that he is a fine young man, do you not?"

Cassie left Ike to answer Esther's question. He spoke slowly. "Yes, Esther, but not, I think, a young man who will become one of our faith, as I had hoped when I made this plan."

"I could have told thee that, if thee had asked, Ike." Esther spoke almost proudly. "He is a man of principles that he would not change to marry."

121

"But thy principles are not so strong; is that what thee would say?"

Esther's face fell. "It is not that, Ike. It is that I do not feel our discipline is just when it makes such rules. If I must find some other church with Thomas, I will do it."

Ike sighed. "Well, Esther, thee knows it will make trouble with thy parents, that it will go hard with them."

"With thee and them, too, Ike, since thee has asked Thomas here. I am afraid thee will be blamed for this. But I will speak to Father and to Mother. I want them to know that thee had naught to do with the start of this, that my mind was settled before ever I told thee."

Then with a defiance Ike had not seen in her, Esther added, "And I tell thee now, Uncle Ike, that regardless of what the meeting does, I *will not say I am sorry* for marrying Thomas, not even to get back into the meeting! They may send their committees to me, but it will be of no avail. Thee would never say thee was sorry thee had married Cassie, Ike; thee knows that!"

"But that is not the same, Esther. Cassie *is* of the meeting."

Esther did not answer, but went slowly to bed, still excited from the evening with Thomas, but plainly no less worried about what her parents and the meeting would do.

The next evening Cassie and Esther had scarcely finished the dishes when Samuel and Priscilla opened the door and entered. When first they spoke, Cassie could see that they must have heard something about Thomas. And their indignation was not all directed at Esther, though their glances at her were dark.

Ike spoke gravely and offered them chairs. Samuel remained standing. Priscilla sat down beside her daughter on the daybed.

Samuel seemed undecided where best to attack. At last he said, a little loudly, "Well, Esther, what has thee to say for thyself? Thee knows what I mean. Thee has become the talk of the neighborhood with thy secret meetings."

Cassie felt anger rising in her, anger that a father should accuse his daughter without asking her first for her side of the story. She restrained the words that came to her lips. This was Ike's brother, and the matter was one for the Evans family, not one in which she should mix, unless through her loyalty and love for Esther she should be forced to take her side.

Esther stood, and Cassie thought wonderingly that she looked as the books described the Greek goddesses, with a kind of flame about her and a glance at her father as stern and unafraid as his own. Esther waited for him to continue, but he stared at her flashing eyes in astonishment. He was not used to such an attitude from his children.

Esther's voice was low and controlled. "Thee believes all thee hears about thy daughter without asking? Thee does not say, 'There is an evil report about thee; it is not true, is it, my daughter?' No, thee accuses me with thy very tone!"

Samuel stepped back, almost as if he feared this girl who answered him so unflinchingly. "Well, speak, then!" he demanded. "Is it true?"

"The words are perhaps true, that I have had secret meetings with Thomas, but the hints in thy tone are not true. I have done nothing of which thee need be ashamed, as thee should know."

Now Ike spoke. "The meetings were not all secret. Last evening Thomas Keith was here for supper, here as a friend of Father and Mother Ballinger. We wished to know this young man—" Ike paused, then said deliberately, "to whom Esther is about to engage herself."

"Thee means to stand there and tell me, Ike, that thee would ask this young man to thy house—against our wishes? Thee is getting to be too much influenced to do things of which thee knows the meeting would not approve." Samuel seemed relieved that now he could direct his wrath at someone besides his daughter, whose manner had become so embarrassing to him. He turned to Ike with more assurance.

Cassie could be quiet no longer. "Thee means influenced by the Ballingers, doubtless, Samuel. Thee refers to my father, I have no doubt."

"If the shoe fits thee, then wear it."

Well, Samuel had the last word there. While Cassie was searching for an answer, Ike spoke in warning. "Samuel, I will not—"

Esther's voice rang out in the room. "Father, thee has said too much already! Cassie and Ike had only my best interests in mind. They wished to see and judge if Thomas is a worthy young man, or if thy daughter is being deceived by a scoundrel. Thee shall not blame them that they did a kindness to me."

Then suddenly, to Cassie's astonishment, Esther dropped the tone and manner of Christian brotherhood. "I tell you now, both of you, that I will marry Thomas; neither you nor the meeting can stop me, if he is willing. And if he should refuse to marry me because my parents do not consent, then I shall go and beg him—" her voice rang even louder in the room until Cassie felt, rather than thought, alarm that John should be wakened, "for the Lord has shown us both that we were meant for each other. What God hath joined together, let no man put asunder. And God would not reveal this to both of us if it were not meant to be."

Samuel's face was red; Priscilla wiped her eyes on a handkerchief. Then a new idea came to Samuel. "Get thy clothes; thee will go home with us where thee will not be out meeting this young man, where we can see what thee is doing, and no one will be encouraging disobedience."

"No, I will *not* go with you. And I think you will not try to take me against my will."

No, Cassie thought admiringly, Samuel would not try that. Esther looked as if she would bite and scratch her father, were he to put a hand on her. What would Ike do? Cassie held her breath while she waited for Ike's decision, and held her tongue as well.

His voice was like steel, as cold and as sharp. "Thee is the one who had best go, Samuel. Thee has insulted thy daughter, thy sister-in-law, and her parents. That seems enough for one evening. Thee had best go before I forget that thee is my brother and that Friends do not lift their hands against their brothers, for I fear I have taken all I can from thee."

Priscilla spoke through her tears. "Let us go now, Samuel. Let us meditate on this before more harm is done."

Samuel seemed glad of an excuse not to answer and followed Priscilla quickly from the house.

Esther's voice was shaken. "I'm sorry, Ike, that I should bring thee such grief. I feared that thee would be blamed for this, that I would cause thee trouble if thee helped me."

"Thee knows," Ike said, "that we, too, are sorry that thee must marry out of the meeting. But we see that thee is determined, and thy young man seems a worthy person, in spite of his beliefs. Thee will find thyself cut off from thy family, but I see thee will not let that hold thee back. But thee will always be welcome here and, I am sure, at Father Ballinger's."

"Thank thee, Ike. Thee may be sure thee will always have our deep gratitude and affection, both thee and Cassie." She added sadly, "Thee is very fortunate, Ike, to have found someone so good for thee in the meeting, for I think thee would have married Cassie even if she had not been."

Ike did not answer, but Cassie thought that Esther was right.

NOT LONG AFTER THEY HAD GONE TO BED, CASSIE KNEW THAT THE baby would soon arrive. Perchance the evening's excitement had brought on her labor. Ike looked so tired that she was tempted to wait longer before rousing him, yet Esther would not be experienced enough to deliver the baby alone. She sent Ike on his way for Mother, but did not wake Esther. Ike would stop and ask Lizzie Elliott to come, lest Mother not get there in time.

Cassie felt very knowledgeable this time, not in the least afraid, as she had been before.

Lizzie came quickly, and since everything was ready, Lizzie sat beside Cassie's bed, and they talked while they waited. Lizzie was a good woman, sober and kind, but she, too, had heard rumors about Esther. She said quietly, "Samuel's Esther is here?"

"Yes, but I thought not to waken her unless we should need her. She was tired when she went to bed."

Cassie felt that Lizzie would have been glad to talk of Esther's problem, but unless Cassie brought the matter up, she would not mention it. And Cassie was not ready to discuss it with anyone outside the family.

By the time Mother and Ike returned, the pains were very hard and close. Ike sat beside the bed, and Cassie held his hand very tightly, trying not to let him know how truly bad the pains were. Then, knowing it could not be long, she said, "Thee will just be in the way now, Ike; thee had better go and keep the fire burning brightly."

His face was white and his tone low. "It seems wrong that thee must do it all, that I can in no way help thee."

"Thee helps by loving me, Ike. But this is woman's work, and we will get along all right." She kissed him and hid the pain from his eyes as he left the room.

Lizzie and Mother were very busy. The doctor they had had before was with a patient on the far side of the county, and Cassie had said there was no use in trying to find another. Had not the doctor said that Mother could do as well as he?

It was not long before Mother called Ike in to see the tiny red-haired girl lying beside Cassie. Dressed in a long gown, already the child had something of Cassie in her face, a look that seemed half mischievous.

Ike gazed down at them both and said gently, "Two Cassies, now. I never thought to be so lucky as to get a daughter so like thee. Let us name her Cassie."

"No, let us call her Caroline. That is somewhat like Cassie, but will not confuse us. When thee calls me, I do not always want thy daughter to come running."

"As thee wishes, Cassie."

Since Esther was there, and seemed likely to stay until her marriage to Thomas, Mother was free to go home after the first two days. Esther was used to caring for children, and Ike had some time now to help, so everything went well. John was a good little boy, seeming older than his two years, but from the beginning Caroline was more trouble than her brother.

Soon Cassie was feeling stronger, but she was glad that Esther could be there to help her. Esther and Thomas would not marry at once. Ike had explained to Thomas the stand of his brother and his wife, and Thomas had agreed that there seemed naught else to do but be married without their consent.

Esther's hope chest, full of the things she had made and helped her mother make since her childhood, sat at home and would continue to sit there. Esther had said firmly, "I will not take from them the things they do not wish to give. I will make more during this winter." Ike had insisted that she must be paid for her work, though she asked only enough to buy material to make linens to replace the ones she would not get from her home.

Mother Ballinger came often to help, and the three of them made quilts, hemmed sheets, and finished tablecloths. Soon there was enough so that Esther need not be ashamed when she became Thomas's wife.

One night after Esther had gone to bed, Cassie said sadly to Ike, "It would be nice if we could have an infare for Esther and Thomas. Does thee think it would make thy family even more angry than they are now?"

"I think we had best not do that, Cassie. Already we have defied them by allowing her to be with us. Soon I think the committee will call on us, but I am ready when they come."

Cassie did not ask Ike what he would say to them, but she was confident he would not retreat from the stand he had taken with Samuel.

Because of the new baby, the committee did not come at once; yet it was not many days before there was a knock at the door. Looking from the kitchen window, Cassie saw the horses of the Friends chosen to deal with them. The words used in the business meeting, "to deal with offenders," flashed through her mind.

To the Ballingers this did not bear such a strange and unusual sound, but Ike was not used to being an offender before the meeting. Cassie would not have been surprised had she herself been the cause for such a visit, but for one of Samuel's family to be at fault somehow lessened the blow for both of them.

Before opening the door to the committee, Ike said quickly, "Esther, thee had better see if John is sleeping. This will not be pleasant for thee."

At first Esther hesitated, and Cassie feared that she would insist on staying to face the committee. Then she turned quickly and left the room.

Friends Eli Cox and Ezra Newby entered and were seated at Ike's invitation, and Cassie restrained a smile at their discomfort. They seemed hurried, as though they wished to deal with this unpleasant task and be through. Ike's virtue was too much respected for their duty to be easy for them. Cassie wondered if it could also be that they feared her own likeness to her father, who was able to defend himself well, to back his argument with Scripture. Cassie knew she must guard her tongue this time. It would be best for Ike to speak and for her to listen.

Eli Cox began. "Ike Evans, we have been appointed to call on thee in regard to a complaint made by thy brother Samuel. He says that thee has encouraged his daughter Esther to marry outside the meeting, that thee has allowed Thomas Keith to visit Esther in thy house."

Ike spoke with great firmness. "Samuel is wrong in saying these things. Esther and Thomas had plighted their troth before we knew anything of it. As Esther's uncle, it seemed to me that it was a better thing that they should meet here, that Cassie and I should become acquainted with this young man she has determined to marry."

Since Eli Cox remained silent, Ike continued, "Though we would not wish for Esther to marry out of the meeting, we can find no fault with Thomas Keith. This is a matter about which I have meditated, and it was revealed to me through the Inner Light that Esther was in need of a friend. As her uncle, I felt it the duty of Cassie and me to be the friends she needed."

He added, "Thee may also tell my brother Samuel that after the marriage has taken place, Cassie and I will hold both Esther and Thomas in friendship as is the place of followers of Christ."

Cassie heard Ike's words with surprise. She knew that Ike believed the Inner Light was the most important part of the

Friends' belief, but he did not usually speak so freely of it.

Cassie could see that her husband's considered statements might well bear more weight than her impulsive answers to the charges. After a short time, Eli Cox and Ezra Newby left. They had made no threat that Ike and Cassie would be asked to leave the meeting.

So the plans for the marriage went on, a marriage that was to be a very quiet one, without the way of making vows that Cassie had thought so beautiful in her own wedding. Esther would feel a little homesickness for the Friends' way of doing things, but she could bear the lesser sorrow for the greater joy of being married to Thomas.

A letter came from Ike's mother, addressed as always to Ike without including Cassie in the salutation. It was a harsh letter, telling Ike he had done wrong in taking Esther's side in such a matter. She said, as Samuel had, that Ike was allowing himself to be influenced and was growing away from the teaching he had learned at his mother's knee.

Ike did not at first hand the letter to Cassie to read as usual. Then, knowing that she might think it even worse than it was, he put it on the table before her.

After Cassie had read it, she took his hand and said gently, "Thee need not worry about what she says about thy wife, Ike. It is not that which pains me, but her reproach to thee, when thee has only done what thee feels to be God's will."

Cassie could see that this comforted Ike, and she was glad that at last he seemed able to ignore his mother's intolerant words, to worry less about his mother's reactions. Cassie said a silent prayer of thankfulness that Mother Evans was so far away from Ike.

When Esther read the letter, she smiled and said, "Grandfather will not feel this way. Sometime I will ask him to come and stay awhile with Thomas and me when we are married. Poor Grandfather, he would find *joy* in being godly if Grandmother would let him. Thee is lucky, Ike, to find thee a wife who thinks it is godly to be happy."

"Thee is right, Esther," Ike replied. "God sometimes sends us greater happiness than we deserve."

Cassie spoke up sharply. "And why would thee think thee did not deserve happiness, Ike? Has thee done aught to make thee undeserving?"

"Cassie, thee knows we all have sinned and fallen short of the glory of God."

Cassie knew that truly she herself sinned daily and fell short of the glory of God. It seemed that she was increasingly impatient these days, even with John, good as he was.

There would soon be much work to do, with the spring labor coming. Esther was helpful but had to attend to her own sewing, and as the wedding came nearer, her head seemed to be in the clouds. Cassie could understand that, but she was sometimes very tired. She feared that she would be even more tired when she must do all of the work herself. Ike would have no time to help her when the need became greatest.

At last, Esther and Thomas were married. Esther had asked Cassie and Ike not to attend, since it would only add fuel to the fire of her father's anger and bring them under more criticism. Cassie and Ike were thankful for Esther's thoughtfulness. Only a short time before, a committee had been sent to labor with some members of the meeting who had attended a marriage contrary to the Friends' discipline. These members had been required to apologize to the meeting for this action.

Surely Cassie and Ike had had enough trouble with the

family and the meeting. The pleasure of attending Esther's wedding would not have compensated for the conflicts it would have caused.

⤙ XVII ⤚

ESTHER CAME OFTEN AND HELPED CASSIE, AND THOMAS WOULD come over in time to take Esther home. In spite of his learning and the pleasure he found in Father's company, Thomas seemed to find in Ike a friend of his own age, one who could help him in this strange new way of life. To Ike this was a never-ending cause for wonder. He could not see why Thomas, who was so educated and as given to reading as Father and Cassie, should have such apparent respect for his opinions.

Where farming was concerned, Thomas's deference did not surprise Ike, but in matters of politics, of ethics, and of philosophy, Thomas listened with respect to the statements Ike made. Although reluctant at first, Ike began to speak with increasing freedom as he understood that Thomas felt his ideas good—better perhaps than those of Father, who was so ready to express himself that sometimes a wild idea became an opinion before he had considered it carefully.

Once Thomas said to Ike, "If all the Friends were like you, Ike, I could well join them, and Esther could go back to the meeting she loves." Esther looked at him quickly.

To Cassie's joy, Ike borrowed books from Thomas and read them more willingly than when Cassie had tried to force him to read. This new friendship for Ike and the sisterly relationship Cassie had with Esther became an increasing happiness to the four of them.

There was a drought that summer, and the well that was to have been dug had to be postponed again. There was no money to pay for help, so Ike would have to clear more of the land himself.

During the long dry days, Cassie often found herself and the children drinking water that was stale and brackish. Even Father hesitated to blame Ike this time for the delay. Whether it was because he understood the reasons and so could not censure Ike, or whether he feared Cassie's anger, which in her tiredness was more easily aroused, Cassie could not decide.

Father's restraint seemed to make Cassie's impatience with Ike's slowness in keeping his promise of the well even greater. If she could have taken this impatience out on Father, she might have been more able to forgive Ike.

At last the summer ended and with it the drought. Now there was plenty of rain water in the barrels by the house. Ike had more time to help her with the children, and she felt a great shame as she remembered how cruel she had sometimes been to Ike and how patient he had been with her.

The autumn had never seemed so good. She took the children out to the field where Ike shucked corn and watched him, John sometimes pulling the shucks from an ear and throwing it high in the wagon. Caroline was either a very good and happy child or a very bad one. Mother Ballinger once said, "She is much the kind of child thee was, Cassie—full of smiles or tears."

Caroline could now walk and run about the little house, pulling things down from the tables, while John went behind replacing them, trying to help his busy mother.

Christmas came and was a great happiness, with the two children gazing in wonder at a tree Ike had brought in from the forest. It was hung with the little gifts they were able to afford and the richer presents from Father and Mother. Thomas and Esther brought small gifts for the children, and on Christmas afternoon, they went to visit Father and Mother Ballinger.

One gift for Mother seemed to Cassie the most wonderful thing she had ever seen for woman: a sewing machine. She had read of these machines, but mother's was the first in the community.

"Oh, Mother, did thee ever think thee would have such a fine thing? Now thee will be through with thy sewing almost before thee starts!"

In Cassie's mind was the almost evil thought that it was she who had need of such a machine, not Mother, who did not find the great need to sew that she had had when Father was more active and Cassie herself was small. Of course Mother would sew for John and Caroline, but Ike did not approve of Mother doing too much of this.

Father watched Cassie as she looked at the machine and said when Ike could not hear him, "Thee knows, Cassie, that I would like to buy thee one like it, if thee would let me. But thee is almost as hardheaded as Ike when it comes to these things. I would have ordered thee one, too, only I knew thy husband would not let thee accept it."

"Oh, Father, thee is good to wish to do it, but thee is very wrong to tempt me so. Not even the well—" Cassie spoke before she thought, for the well was not mentioned these days between them. "Not even the well would be more help to me than this. The man who invented this is truly a benefactor to women."

"Not altogether, Cassie. I read in the paper that this machine has taken the food from the mouths of many spinsters and widows in the East, who now are deprived of the work by which they gained their livelihood. Indeed, Miss Beecher has helped many of these unmarried women by assisting them in starting schools in the West, where they also find husbands. All because of this same invention."

"Then if they find husbands because of it, and their husbands are good, it is still a benefactor. Thee has crossed thyself up in thy argument, Father."

During this interchange with Father, Cassie put out of her mind the covetousness she had felt for this machine. How could she wish for more, when she had Ike and John and Caroline? But it seemed her work was never done now, even though it was easier than it had been in the summer.

She tried very hard to get her mending and sewing done, to knit the stockings for the children and the socks for Ike, before it was time for Ike's busy season. Mother begged Cassie to bring her sewing over and do it on the machine, and Cassie did this as much as she could. But there were times when she could not. It was not possible to carry two children on the horse and the sewing also.

There was, too, a matter of pride. She was not now a young girl who could ask her mother to do the things she should do herself.

After a time, Cassie began to be rested, to feel that she had her duties well in hand and that she was ready for the spring and summer work, which would soon be here.

With her new well-being, Cassie resolved that Second Month should be a kind of vacation for all of them. She and Ike would be gay, read, play with the children, and be rested for the new season.

Ike seemed to have a new kind of gaiety, partly from her new zest, and partly from his companionship with Thomas. Esther and Thomas came often, and Cassie and Esther knitted while Thomas and Ike did the chores that could be brought in before the fire. Ike made Caroline a chair like the one he had made for John. They ate apples and popcorn and hickory nuts cracked before the fire. Cassie felt good in her soul, free of the evil impatience that seemed to go with her tiredness when there was more to do than she could get done.

Then in Fourth Month, Cassie knew there was to be yet another child. Cassie wanted a large family, but if she could not cope with the children she had without being worn and impatient, perhaps it would be better if their family remained small. Yet after her winter's surcease and the rest and holiday she had found in Second Month, she felt able to enjoy this new child, who would come in Eleventh Month.

Esther also was to become a mother. They could sew and plan together. Ike said, a little slowly, "Cassie, of course it is good to have a fine family, but thee must not work so hard as thee did after Caroline was born. I think thee was too tired; this time thee must find a way to save thyself."

So happy was Cassie that she did not even think, "A well, Ike, and allow Father to give me the machine for sewing he would willingly give."

Suddenly it was summer, and Ike seemed never to have enough time for his work. Cassie was strong and well, her work seemed easier than it had been last summer, and the children were less trouble in some ways. Last summer Caroline had still been at her breast, and doubtless this had been a drain on Cassie's strength. Carrying the baby this time seemed good for her.

They had no companionship now with Samuel and Priscilla, and it seemed that Ike missed the contact. For this reason, he had begun to trade work with his brother Wesley. Cassie liked Wesley's wife Rachel in many ways, though they had little real pleasure in each other's company, except for talk of cooking and canning, sewing and quilting.

Wesley and Samuel were much alike, and it might have been

for this reason that they did not always get along well together. Cassie often thought it strange that they should both be so much like Mother Evans in their way of thinking, yet be so glad to go so far away from her. It was good that Ike at least was kind and gentle like Father Evans.

The summer passed, and now Caroline was two and John four. Cassie was less light on her feet and less swift with her work. Again great stacks of sewing and mending piled up.

Though the crops this year were better than last, there was still no time or money for the new well. Yet Cassie, in her great sense of well-being and health, did not feel as rebellious as she had the summer before. Ike could not help it if he did not have money to hire the work done or time to do it himself. When he did have time, it always seemed that the ground was frozen.

She knew it was no sign of lack of love with Ike. He did so many things for her that no other husband in the community did for his wife. Even after five years of marriage, when Cassie thought of him in the field, a feeling of warmth came over her, and she longed to see his figure advancing over the hills of the pasture land.

When Eleventh Month arrived, Cassie knew it would not be long until time for this new baby. This time she could not have Esther. But when Ike and Wesley finished shocking the corn, Ike would have time to help her, to be there to call Mother and Lizzie, as had become almost a custom after the bearing of the two other children.

Cassie wakened heavily one morning. When she was awake enough to know where she was, it took still a little time for her to be aware of Ike beside her, so big and comforting, and of John and Caroline sleeping quietly in the spool bed across the braided rug which she had made the winter before with Esther's help.

She prayed silently, "Dear God, give me strength and wisdom

this day to do Thy will. And, God, would Thee please help me to find time to get my mending done before the baby comes."

Slowly Cassie turned her cumbersome body and carefully put her feet on the floor. She must not fall now, or she might do harm to both herself and the baby. She remembered that today Wesley and Rachel would be here, Wesley to help with shocking the corn, and Rachel and her two youngest children to visit.

She thought of what Rachel had said on their last visit when speaking of the coming of the new baby, "Cassie, thee should not encourage Ike to be so loving. Men—"

Cassie smiled a contented little smile. Only she and Ike knew that, in spite of Ike's outward composure, he needed no encouragement to be loving. His long and solemn upper lip hid a very loving and—what his brothers prayed daily to be delivered from —a very "carnal nature."

She dressed with haste under her full white gown. John or Caroline might soon waken, as they sometimes did in the early morning. Then she laid a gentle hand on Ike's sleeping form and said softly, "Ike, Ike, thee must get up. See, it is already day."

Ike moved under the patchwork quilt. Then he put forth a long arm and pulled Cassie down beside him. In this half-wakeful state, Ike was so much more naturally loving that Cassie was hard put to restrain him.

"No, Ike, thee must get up. I have let thee sleep too long now. Wesley will be here early to help thee with the corn shocking."

Somewhat subdued, Ike said, "Cassie, thee should have called me to build the fire and have it warm for thy getting up. Thee must take care of thyself."

As Cassie began her chores, she thought proudly of Ike's loving nature. Rachel's children came quite as frequently as

Cassie's, though Cassie was sure that Rachel discouraged Samuel's loving nature and encouraged him constantly to struggle to overcome his carnal spirit. Cassie's and Ike's way seemed no more apt to bring children and was much more pleasant. They had great joy in their children, both of them good, though Caroline was oftentimes mischievous. Cassie tried always to remember what Mother had said about Caroline's likeness to herself.

Cassie was already shaking down the wood stove when she heard Ike's reproachful tones. "Cassie, did thee not patch my other shirt? Thee saw the hole in the elbow when thee washed it."

"Ike, I am sorry. Can thee not wear the one thee wore yesterday? Thee remembers that yesterday I worked on the new dress for Caroline." Wesley and Rachel must not see Ike's shirt with the hole in it. Already they found Cassie lacking in many wifely duties.

"Does thee want thy husband to smell like the barn, Cassie? Thee knows that yesterday I hauled out the manure from the stables."

Yes, Cassie knew. Because of the smell, she had brought out his second-best shirt for the evening meal.

"Put on thy dirty one, and I will mend thy clean one while thee eats."

The milking done, Ike ate while Cassie mended, hastily ere the children woke and must be dressed. Cassie handed Ike the shirt, its patch a little drawn. She did not remind him that her father had wished to buy her a sewing machine. But she was proud that Father had not dared suggest it to Ike himself, knowing what his reply would be: "Father Ballinger, thee sees I can provide for my family."

Cassie had scant time for her own breakfast and had scarcely wiped out the dishpan when the wagon rattled in. Rachel was on the seat beside Wesley, and their two youngest ones were on a pile of straw in the back.

Cassie went out as quickly as her bulk would allow and greeted Rachel with affection. "Good morning to thee, Rachel, and to thee, Wesley. Becca, Elijah, do come in. John and Caroline can hardly wait to see you."

The morning went almost before Cassie realized it. She was uncommonly slow, but with Rachel's help, dinner was ready when Wesley and Ike came in.

When the last dish was dried and put in the tin safe with the patterned nail holes on the door, Rachel said, "Thee is tired, Cassie. I will sweep the floor, and thee shall rest thyself."

"Thank thee, Rachel," Cassie replied gratefully. "If thee will, I can mend and sew a little while I rest."

Rachel's eyes were kind as she saw the tiny white dresses with their full, hand-sewn ruffles. "Thee makes very neat baby clothes, Cassie."

Cassie's smile was regretful. "But not neat mending for Ike. I have had much practice with baby clothes, and I enjoy such sewing. But Ike's shirts and coats—oh, I seem never to get so I can do them well and swiftly, as I must to get them done. And soon John will be wearing clothes like his father's."

"Thee will learn, Cassie. Thee is so impatient." She sighed. "When thee has four grown sons and six other children, thee will be more skillful and swift, thee may be sure."

Somehow Cassie expected and dreaded Rachel's next remark. "Thy mother has a machine for sewing, Priscilla tells me."

Why could Ike's family not take pleasure in the good fortune of others without the covetousness, which they would be quick to deny, showing through?

"Yes, it is very useful." Then, carried away in spite of the caution she had laid on her tongue, Cassie said, "Oh, Rachel, thee must go and see it! It is a fine thing. Such a friend to womankind."

"I suppose thee will want one, too."

Cassie felt her defenses rising. Rachel had been too long married to an Evans to see any but the Evanses' way of looking at a thing. Not in a hundred years of marriage into the Evans family would Cassie become like that.

"Any woman would want one if she were able to have it."

"Wesley says they are worldly; that it is woman's nature to sit and sew. Thee said thyself thee could rest while thee sewed."

Cassie's voice grew tight and almost angry. "Thee must not say my father is a worldly man."

"Cassie, thee knows I did not mean that."

"We had best talk of something else."

The rest of the afternoon was not the joy the morning had been. Even the children seemed more quarrelsome. Cassie wanted to take John's and Caroline's small chairs away from Becca, who was being too rough with them, but was as quickly ashamed of herself. Truly the spirit of contention was always close, waiting to rise and take control of her nature.

She went to the stone jar filled with cookies and gave the children some to make up for the evil thoughts she had had. She struggled with her resentment and made her voice warm and affectionate to Rachel so that she would carry away no hard feeling.

But at supper after Wesley and Rachel had gone, Cassie was quiet, too quiet. Ike looked at her closely. "What is it, Cassie?" His voice was worried. "Thee did not quarrel with Rachel?"

"Thee should know I would not quarrel with Rachel."

"I only wondered. Before they left, Rachel was less given to talking than is her nature. And thee too seems very queer tonight."

Cassie made no answer. But when the children were in bed and she sat down to mend, the words seemed to come out by themselves.

"Thy family thinks my father a worldly man."

"Cassie!" exclaimed Ike in dismay. "What has Rachel said to thee?"

"That a sewing machine is a worldly thing; that I, too, might wish one. So she thinks me worldly, too."

Ike's long upper lip was set firmly against his lower one.

"Ike, does thee think me worldly?"

"Cassie, thee knows I could not marry and cherish a woman that I thought worldly."

"But, Ike, thee knows I *do* wish a machine—so that thy clothes may be neatly made, so that the stitches in thy shirts may be even and strong."

"Thee is sometimes wrong, Cassie, though never worldly."

"Ike, thee is usually a wise and careful man, even with thy opinions. Father said the other day that Thomas Keith had told him he thought thee a very wise young man, one of the wisest he had ever known. Yet thee is like to form an opinion without pondering on it, if thy family be in agreement."

Ike looked at Cassie sharply. As Cassie knew, Ike prided himself on his considered opinions. Even his family was not allowed to set out his beliefs. Cassie kissed Ike good night; the rancor she had felt eased a little.

⌐XVIII⌐

At midnight cassie was awakened by the twinge that heralded the now familiar process of nature. Calmly she awakened Ike. "Thee must go for my mother, Ike. It is time for the baby."

In this at least, Ike was not as calm as Cassie. She thought a little grimly that Ike could not accept nature in any of its forms as easily as she. Yet neither could he accept new machines as well as she.

"Will thee be all right while I am gone, Cassie?"

"All will be well, Ike. Though thee might stop and ask Lizzie to come and stay with me, if thee would be easier. It will take thee some time."

Ike's fingers were thumbs, and Cassie found herself comforting him as she fastened the frayed buttonholes in his coat.

She watched him from the window as he drove off swiftly in the light wagon. He could have gone more quickly on the horse, but it would be better if Father did not have to drive Mother over. Father was apt to be much in the way at a time like this. He could, of course, be sent for the doctor to make him feel useful, though the baby would probably arrive before the doctor did, as had happened before.

Cassie was glad to hear Lizzie's voice at the door. Cassie's babies came quickly and, according to Priscilla and Rachel, with much ease.

Lizzie carried Caroline and John to the daybed in the living room, where they would not be bothered or awakened. Everything was in readiness when she heard Ike drive in with Mother.

When Ike stood awkwardly near, trying to help, Cassie said firmly, "Thee look after the fire and the children, Ike. All will be taken care of."

Indeed, it was not long before Lizzie went in to tell Ike that this time there was a boy. The baby was bathed and dressed and lay in the warm curve of Cassie's tired body. Ike stood looking down at the two of them with tears in his eyes.

Cassie forced a wan smile and whispered weakly, "Thee need not be so sober, Ike. Thee is lucky. Thee has a son waiting for thee."

He pulled the soft blanket back and gazed at his son. "He has thy mouth, Cassie, though his hair is dark."

"Thee may kiss thy son's mother, Ike." To make him smile, she added, "And say thank thee for another hand on thy farm."

His face was full of love as he kissed her, though with Lizzie and Mother watching, the kiss was a little stiff. Mother said, "Thee had better get thee a daughter next, Cassie. Thee could use a hand in thy house."

Cassie replied with a tired laugh, "Yes, another daughter, or a sewing machine."

Ike either did not hear or ignored her remark.

Since Enos Elliott had done Ike's chores, Ike sat down to the breakfast Lizzie had prepared. Before eating, he thanked God for the son He had sent and for Cassie's well-being.

Cassie could scarcely wait the four days her mother ordered before she was up and about. It was good to be slim and light again, to be able to stoop and bend in comfort, to feel herself small in Ike's arms.

It was pleasant to have her mother with her, but it would be good, too, to be alone with her family again. Mother would understand, so Cassie had no feeling of disloyalty because of her thought. At the end of the week, Cassie said, "Father will need thee at home, Mother. Thee must not slight him for me."

Mother looked at her keenly. "Is thee sure, Cassie, that thee is ready to take charge again? Thee remembers that thee was very tired after Caroline was born. Thee did not come back to thy strength as thee did with John. Thy father is willing for me to stay until thee is rested and well; thee knows that."

Cassie said quickly, "I know, Mother, but Ike is through with the hard work now, and he can help. Thee knows thee is homesick to be with Father, that he depends on thee."

Mother answered, still doubtful, "Yes, that is true. But it will not hurt thy father to learn to depend on himself a little. I feel thee needs me longer."

It was decided that Mother should stay until Third Day before leaving Cassie, and as Cassie finished bathing the baby for the second time, she was suddenly very glad that Mother had not taken her at her word and left her to Ike's ministrations. She wished that Esther could be with her again.

But her strength came back quickly this time, and she mended and rested a great deal while Mother was still there. Mother left with some reluctance and also with a stack of sewing, which she took in spite of Cassie's feeling that Ike might not approve. She had not forgotten his hint that she was a little selfish with Mother.

Soon little Elias was smiling from the cradle, and Cassie saw that he was to be a good baby, more like John than Caroline. This would be a blessing, as there was less time for his care.

This time Father and Mother came to visit Cassie and Ike for Christmas, since the baby was so small and the weather bad. Cassie could feel an atmosphere of love here that she had seen in few other houses. She felt it in her own parents' home, of course, and in Thomas and Esther's. But in many houses there was too much worry about the getting and keeping of money and too little thought about the great blessings God had given. But then few families were so blessed with health and children —and love—as was her own.

Cassie thought a little wistfully of the machine Father had given Mother last Christmas and of his wish to give her one, too. But she would not spoil Ike's pleasure in the small gifts they could afford by bringing up such a sore subject.

New Year's passed, and suddenly Cassie realized that it would soon be spring. Ike would no longer be able to help her. She began to work at her sewing with a new zeal, to make, while she still had time, the clothes the children must have. But as she devoted her time to the making of clothes, the mending fell far behind.

Ike, too, must have new shirts, and she saw one day, as she took his long underdrawers from the line, that they were patched beyond redemption. The making of new underdrawers was a chore she must somehow find time to do.

One morning as Ike dressed before the fireplace, he slipped his long foot into the leg of his drawers, and it came out at the knee. As he stood there looking in exasperation at the ragged drawers, Cassie was almost overcome with an urge to burst into laughter. Ike, so solemn, in such a ludicrous position. She turned away quickly lest he see her merriment. This he would not find funny.

He said, "Cassie, does thee want a girl to help thee? Thy sewing—"

Controlling her merriment, she answered him with apparent soberness. "So thee would prefer a comely girl to a sewing machine? Thee thinks she would be nicer to have around thy house, would perchance be less worldly, more in the nature of things?"

Cassie saw from the look on Ike's face that she had gone beyond Ike's limit both in humor and in self-control. *This* was not a thing about which Ike could jest.

"Cassie! Thee knows better than to say such things! Thee should be chastised!" Ike's voice came in a roar, a tone Cassie had never heard from him and had never thought to hear directed at herself.

His hand rose, and there was a small clap as it struck Cassie's cheek—small indeed, but to Cassie it sounded like the clap of doom itself.

"Never, *never* say such things to me!"

Still enraged, Ike finished dressing with a speed unlike him and strode from the room.

Cassie stood, holding her cheek, unable to move, and her eyes slowly filled with tears. Ike had struck her! Oh, no, not Ike! What had she said? How had she said it? As her words came back to her, horror suddenly changed into understanding, and she sank weakly into a chair.

She should have known better than to say such things to Ike. It had been hard enough for him to become reconciled to what he still half believed to be his carnal nature. Yet to suggest, even in jest, that Ike would allow this nature to tempt him to take pleasure in another woman! Indeed, Cassie should have known that she had overstepped.

Too late she remembered Priscilla's telling her that Ike, when angry, was an Ike she would not recognize, that Ike himself would not recognize. Though he was slow to anger, he was terrible when his wrath was aroused. There was a limit past which one should not go with him. Cassie herself had seen it reached in Ike's words to Samuel about Esther.

What should she do? Had it been Cassie, she would by now have been over her anger, repentant. She was apt to punish the children quickly and mildly, and they, used to her swift impatience, did not hold it against her. She was glad the children were still abed and had not seen this thing. If Ike could so forget himself, surely even their presence would not have restrained him.

She knew not how to judge or deal with Ike's rage. Perhaps he would not cool quickly from such a fire, since he did not readily acquire such heat.

Cassie would gladly have gone to Ike to tell him that she herself was to blame. She would have asked his forgiveness for the thing she had said. But, if she should forgive him without his asking, it might only make him more repentant and less able to forgive himself.

So Cassie began to prepare breakfast and to make out the biscuits, wondering all the while if Ike would be able to eat. Poor Ike! She would make him understand that this was something she could forget, even if he could not.

From the window she saw him coming with the milk. His steps were slow, his eyes on the ground. It seemed an hour before he reached the back door and stepped inside. Setting the bucket on the kitchen table, he came to her, his hands hanging limply at his sides.

To Cassie his voice was like the sound of weeping. "Cassie, Cassie, can thee ever forgive me? Oh, Cassie!"

At the sight of the tears in Ike's eyes, Cassie flew to him and on tiptoe covered his grieving face with her kisses.

"Thee knows, Cassie, my wit is not light. Thy words seemed like blasphemy. Thee should not speak lightly of such things. Thee knows there could be no one but thee."

"I know, Ike. Not again will I make mock of thee."

ᴖ⟨ XIX ⟩ᴖ

ALL MORNING CASSIE TRIED TO SHOW IKE WITH LOVING WORDS and deeds that she did not hold against him the thing he had done, that it was over and done with, never to be remembered again.

But she could see him scourging himself. He would stand

and look at her as she went about her tasks, offering to help in ways he would never have considered before. After a while she took his arm and led him over to the daybed and seated herself beside him there.

"Ike, does thee remember the times I have nagged thee, have been impatient and short of speech with thee?"

"Thee is *never*, Cassie. Thee is the best wife man ever had."

"See, thee has forgotten already. When thee has only once been unkind to me, thee thinks I must remember it. If thee can forgive and forget, thee should see that I can also. Thee must quit acting as though thee had done something unforgivable. I will not have it. Now go out and get to thy work, and leave me to mine."

Ike managed a weak smile, then went outdoors. Cassie saw him splitting wood for the kitchen stove. Then he seemed simply to stand around, as though he had not made up his mind what to do next.

Finally, he walked purposefully to the barn and soon came out leading the horse, which he had saddled. Without telling her where he was going, he rode out the driveway, past the schoolhouse, and down the narrow road.

This was not like Ike at all. Usually he told Cassie where he was going and asked whether he could do any errands for her if he was going to Overton.

Nor did he explain when he returned where he had been. Although Cassie was puzzled, she did not ask. But John and Caroline did. "Where did thee go, Father?" Ike did not answer and went out to do the evening chores.

There began to be days with a touch of spring in them, days when Cassie wished to forget that she was the mother of three children and to go out and run down the country road or walk in the newly warm sun. The spring flowers began to push through the thawed ground, and one day John brought in a dandelion.

Ike seemed to have forgiven himself to some extent, though he was even kinder to Cassie and unusually free in showing his love. It was almost like when first they were married and no one was there but her and Ike. The feeling of love around them began to be something so warm and strong it seemed that Cassie could almost reach out and pull it around her like a blanket.

One day Ike mentioned something that Father had said, though Cassie had not known that he had seen Father. The spring rains had made the roads so bad that they had been unable to go to meeting, and Father had not been at their home. She would have paid this less note except that Ike stopped in confusion. When had Ike gone to Father's?

As soon as the roads cleared a little, Ike made a trip to town in the wagon. Cassie presumed he had gone for the groceries they needed. But when the wagon came into sight, the children ran in, calling, "Mother, what has Father brought from Overton? See, there is a box, a big box in the wagon!"

Only the presence of Enos Elliott on the wagon seat beside Ike kept Cassie from running down the road to meet them. Surely there could be but one thing in a box of such a shape!

As they drove into the yard and pulled up in front, Cassie went to the door, hiding with difficulty her eagerness and excitement. Enos and Ike climbed into the back of the wagon and carefully lifted the crate to the porch, where they opened it even more carefully.

As the last board fell away, Ike said, "A sewing machine for thee, Cassie. A gift from thy father."

"Thank thee, Ike! Thank thee!"

"Not me, Cassie. Thank thy father. Thee knows it is not a thing I could afford to buy thee."

With Enos there, Cassie could not tell Ike the things she might have. Yet her smile told him that she knew—and Ike realized that she knew—that it had been a much greater thing for him to allow Father to give her the machine, to go to Father and give his permission, than if he had taken the money from their own meager savings. By bowing his pride in "being beholden to no one," Ike had done his best to make amends for the dreadful thing he felt he had done in his rage.

That night after the children were in bed, Cassie took the drawers she had cut out for Ike the week before and, placing her foot on the treadles, which looked like iron footprints, began to repay him for the sacrifice he had made.

Ike came and stood beside her, watching. At last he said, "Thee was right, Cassie. It is surely a boon to womankind. Thee will not be so hard pressed with thy work now. It is good that sometimes goodness comes from evil." He waited a moment before continuing.

"Thy father is a very understanding man, too. He did not say, 'Why has thee decided now that I may do this thing?' He thanked me for allowing him to do this for thee, as though it were I who did the favor. He is a good and a godly man, Cassie. I would not have thee think I do not admire thy father and respect him because sometimes I have not agreed with him."

Cassie had been so surprised at Ike's making such a long speech that she had stopped her work and gazed at him. When he had finished, she took his hand and rubbed it against her cheek.

"Thee is a good and a just man thyself, Ike. I am proud of you both. If thy sons can be a little like both thee and my father, they will be very fine men."

Cassie found herself so delighted with the new machine that sewing, indeed, became a pleasure to her. Things that earlier she would never have tried to make became easy. First, she finished all the mending to prove to Ike how worthwhile the machine was. Then she made the shirts he had needed for so long. Dresses for Caroline seemed to flow from under the needle.

Finally Mother said to her, "Cassie, thee is so extreme in thy nature. Thee is wearing thyself out and making little lines between thy eyes from so much sewing by candlelight. Thee is not being very wise about this, for thee will be too tired when the hard work of the spring starts."

But Cassie could not listen. The last time Father had gone East, he had brought her a dress length for her birthday. She now resolved that she would make a dress herself and not allow Mother to help. It would have many tucks and flounces, such as she found in the dresses in *Godey's Lady's Book*, which Father had had sent to Mother.

Ike would be proud of her when he saw what she could do. No more need he be ashamed of her lack of sewing skill when his brothers' wives looked at the things she had made. It would be the kind of dress that Priscilla had paid five dollars to have made in Greenbury.

Thus, Cassie sewed, and sometimes ripped out what she had sewed. Mother had helped her cut and fit the dress, for Cassie feared she might spoil the silk if she did this herself. But the sewing would be hers alone.

It would have gone more easily had it not been for Caroline's interest in the project. Also, Cassie had to care for Elias, who was now beginning to sit up, propped against a pillow on a comfort placed on the floor. Elias was beginning to play with the things the children brought him, and Caroline was wont to give him things he should not have. Cassie found herself becoming as impatient and cross as she had been when Caroline was a baby—this time because of her own intemperance, her lack of restraint.

Ike would come in for his supper and find the sewing still spread out on the table. He would patiently help her, though Cassie knew he must be tired, now that the spring plowing had started.

Cassie had begun to run a kind of race with herself. When this dress was done, *then* she would cover the machine and begin to do the things that came with the spring. She would start the garden when Ike got it plowed. She would set the hens, something she knew she should have done two weeks ago. It was time too for housecleaning. What was the matter with her that she could not do things in moderation?

Finally the last button was in place, and Cassie could clear away the litter for good. She had not told Ike it was finished. After the children were in bed, Cassie carefully combed her hair, then tried on the dress for Ike to see. She stood demurely before him, her hands folded in front of her.

"Thee is beautiful, Cassie. And to think thee made it all thyself. No dressmaker could make a better one."

"Now, Ike, thee need not be ashamed that thy wife cannot do the things thy sisters-in-law can do, the things thy mother would have in thy wife."

"But, Cassie, I was never ashamed of thee! Did thee work so hard and sacrifice thyself for that?"

Suddenly it came to Cassie that she had sacrificed, not herself, but her children and Ike for a foolish resentment.

How much harder it was to learn life's lessons than to learn to sew and to mend. Well, she would remember when she wore the dress that she had been wrong—and vain! "Vanity of vanities, all is vanity, saith the preacher." There were all kinds of vanity, it seemed.

Cassie found that, because of her neglect, she must now throw herself into the other kinds of work that were needful and pushing. The garden was ready to be planted, the house to be cleaned, and the hens to be set. At night, Cassie was so tired that she could scarcely wait for supper to be over so that she could go to bed. Her old impatience attacked her once more, and she fought a losing battle against it.

The children seemed to feel their mother's unrest and to catch it from her. Even John, who so seldom caused her trouble, became resentful at her crossness and was not saucy, but sullen. Caroline answered her back, and even Elias, who was always such a good baby, cried with the colic. This was doubtless caused by Cassie's overwork and its effect on her milk.

Only once in a while did Cassie feel that sense of a blanket of love around her and her family. What had she done; what was she doing? She prayed that she might become wiser, might be able to restrain her quick words, might learn the limit of her strength and not to go beyond it. Cassie thought of her mother's serenity and prayed for the Inner Light that brought such peace.

One morning Ike hitched up the wagon and took Cassie and the children to spend the day with Esther and her baby, saying she needed a rest and change, and the work must wait. Cassie was grateful for his thoughtfulness, though she wondered if losing a day's work would really be of help to her. But she found the respite good and came back more ready to do her work.

ALMOST BEFORE IT SEEMED POSSIBLE, IT WAS TIME FOR THE threshers. As usual, the weather was hot. It seemed too bad that

Ike should have to work so hard at such a time, and Cassie, also, had much to do to get ready. Ike must not be shamed by an untidy house when they fed the men of the neighborhood. Also, many of their wives would come to help Cassie and to make a social gathering out of what might otherwise be an unpleasant duty.

Everything that could be prepared ahead without danger of spoilage was done the day before. The bread was now ready to go into the oven, and the pickles and jellies had been carried up from the cellar.

Cassie looked around the house with the eyes of the neighbor women and did not find much fault. The house seemed very neat, clean, and homelike. It looked like a house where people lived and loved each other. Cassie was not often sharp with John or Caroline if their small shoes made scratches on the legs of the chairs or table. She believed that a home was for living. If a family could not enjoy their house, then it would not be a real home.

The things she prized, gifts Father had bought in the East for her, dishes Mother had brought in the covered wagon when first they came here—these she tried to preserve, hoping that her own daughters would prize them, too.

The children were taking their afternoon naps, including Caroline, who found it hard to fall asleep in the daytime. Cassie sank down for just a moment on the daybed by the door and was suddenly assailed by a great thirst.

She thought a little unhappily that the water would not be cool for the day was so hot. But no doubt it would wet her mouth, if nothing more.

With this thought, she rose wearily, more tired than when she had first sat down, and went to the kitchen. Ike always brought the bucket of water from the Elliotts' at noon.

She reached for the gourd dipper and glanced into the bucket.

To her dismay there was only enough water to cover the bottom, and that was red with iron. Not harmful, to be sure, but nothing that Cassie could drink.

It was the remains of the water Ike had brought that morning before he went to do his work. He had almost forgotten it then, and she had reminded him sharply, even though she had not been as tired as she was now. She had said, "Ike, I think thee wants to forget it," knowing all the time that he did not.

It seemed she had been right to be cross with him, since he could forget again at noon. He knew that today of all days she needed water badly. Father was right about the well, and she had been wrong to refuse to let him have it dug for her. If Ike would not get it for her himself, she should just tell Father to go ahead with it.

Cassie felt a quick sense of shame at this betrayal of her love for Ike. Never before had she even thought she could let Father do this for her, could so humiliate Ike. If she had not been so tired, she would not have thought such a thing.

But now she must go and get the water herself. They could not wait all the afternoon for a drink. She gave a last look at the children sleeping heavily in their beds, though their faces were scarlet and wet with perspiration. They would surely be all right until she returned. John could be depended upon to try to keep Caroline in hand until she could hurry back.

Cassie set off swiftly down the dusty road and could feel the coarse material of her everyday dress becoming wet as she walked. Her hair was heavy and moist, the little curls bursting out from the braid around her face. Her bonnet was hot, so she took it off and swung it by the strings, but then replaced it since her white skin burned quickly.

Lizzie came to the door and greeted her, but Cassie could only force a smile and say, with an effort not to show her anger at Ike, "I left the children alone, asleep, so I'll not have time to visit with thee. Thank thee for the water."

Bent sideways under the weight of the heavy bucket of water, she started off again down the hot road. Ike could carry two full buckets without spilling a drop, but Cassie's impatience seemed to lend itself to the water. She extended her left arm for balance as she walked, but even then the water sloshed over the side. The drops rolled down the smooth track of the hay wagons and formed tiny dust-coated balls.

Her long skirts dragged around her feet, and the coarse material of the dress stuck to her flesh, pulling at her shoulders. It all seemed to work together to make her troubles worse and her spirits lower.

She surely had a right to be indignant at Ike—not angry, for Friends would not allow themselves to be angry. Then she remembered guiltily that Father was apt to smile at the "righteous indignation" which afflicted so many of the Friends. Was this the kind of indignation she felt, not really indignation at all, but just plain anger?

It was hard to remember that Ike was so good and kind, and so overworked that he really had had no time for her well. Cassie tried to forget how tired he had looked when she had made him get up from a dead sleep this morning. It was not good that one should be so tired early in the morning.

But it was hard to be patient for six years! Today seemed too much for Cassie, and she tried not to remember that Ike was so seldom impatient with her, never spoke harshly when she did not get done the things that should be done.

As Cassie walked down the long road, she began to think of the children at home, left there by themselves because of Ike's forgetfulness. She had put the bread and pies in the oven just before leaving, and the stove was very hot. What if they were playing near, and one of them fell against the stove? She hurried a little more.

The bail cut into the palms of her hands, which never became calloused like those of other women, but blistered and healed up, only to blister again. She changed the bucket from one hand to the other and opened and closed her fingers to ease their cramp.

Impatiently she pushed a strand of hair back under her bonnet; even nature seemed to have joined with her other troubles. Why could her hair not stay back as it should, as the hair of a plain woman should? On the other hand, would a woman who really wished to dress plainly have worked as hard as Cassie had in order to finish a dress which, in spite of its color, was not very plain?

She set the bucket down as she came to the fence and loosened the wire that fastened the gate. Ike had built it for her, labored evenings after a hard day's work so that she could feel free in her mind as to Caroline's whereabouts.

Cassie set the bucket inside the gate and turned to fasten the wire tightly. She could hear nothing from the house.

Though John required more sleep, it was not like Caroline to sleep this long. Recently she had begun to climb on the chairs and tables to find what she wanted. It could well be that she was so occupied now.

Quickly Cassie jerked up the bucket, spilling some of the precious water on the ground, and hurried to the door, her uneasiness growing as she drew closer. As she reached the door, she heard a great crash. She stood staring through the screen. This was by far the worst thing that had happened in all this unhappy day.

When Cassie dried the dishes, she always set the table for the next meal. She now saw the whole tableful of dishes lying on the floor, many of them in pieces. Caroline was crouched behind the table, the corner of the everyday cloth still in her hand. Her face was frightened, and her mouth trembled as she started to cry.

Seeing the look on Caroline's face, Cassie was suddenly filled with grief—for Caroline, for herself, and for the lovely things she had prized.

She felt she could not take another step and, setting the bucket on the worn boards of the porch, she sank down on the stoop and allowed the tears to come to her eyes. As she began to sob, the cat came rubbing around her, and she feared that he might stick his nose in the bucket of water for which she had paid so highly. She rose quickly to save it and went in to pick up the pieces.

John came sleepily from the other room and, frightened at seeing Caroline's and his mother's tears, began to cry himself. In spite of her grief, Cassie felt a great rush of love and sympathy for these children. She sat down on a low stool beside them and, with the bottom of her apron, dried their tears and hers, comforting them and herself by the effort.

When they were quiet, Cassie gave them drinks, washed their faces in the cool water, combed their hair, and led them out to play in the shade of the gnarled apple tree.

Then she knelt beside the table to see what was left. The table cover had cushioned the fall of some of the dishes. The sugar bowl and the vinegar cruet were unbroken. But of the five plates which Mother had brought in the covered wagon only two were left. The glass spoon-holder was broken, but it had been a premium with baking powders, and she could get another.

Cassie looked at the pies browning in the oven and thought how much better broken dishes were than burned hands or faces. She remembered with a shudder the scarred and drawn face of a neighbor who had been badly burned as a child. If that had happened to her children, how she would have blamed herself for leaving them alone!

Yet it was not her fault that she had had to go for the water. It was Ike's. As Cassie worked on through the hot afternoon, this thought stayed with her and grew. Her shame at her own anger seemed somehow to have grown into an even greater resentment toward Ike.

To add to her troubles, Cassie ran out of wood for the stove. She went out, and, taking the ax, as she seldom was forced to do, awkwardly split a huge log that Ike had sawed earlier in the season and hauled close to the house. As she carried the pieces in, the rough bark made prints on her white forearms, adding to her feeling of injury and neglect.

John and Caroline came inside, forgetting their grief and fright, wishing the company she usually gave them at this time of day. They hung on her skirts, got into her path, and begged for bread and butter. Impatiently she cut the great loaf of bread, still warm from baking, and spread fresh butter on the thick slices. Its good odor reminded Cassie that she had hardly eaten at noon, so occupied had she been with the tasks yet to do. She cut an extra slice and dropped down in the doorway with them, smiling for the first time since she had put them in bed for their naps.

The warm feeling of love for this troublesome pair came back to her, and she drew them close and felt comforted herself. She should not have thought so badly of Ike.

Soon Cassie felt the pricking of conscience at being idle when so much was yet to be done. She rose and admonished the children, "Now you be good, children, so I can finish the work before your father comes for supper." Rested and refreshed by the food, she went back to her work with renewed energy and only a twinge of shame at her earlier irritation.

The children played happily under the tree with the rag dolls Mother had made for them. Cassie sighed with satisfaction as she took the last pie from the oven. The oozing browness of the berry pies gave her a feeling of pride in the thought that she had made them, had even picked the berries early in the morning from the woods back of the house. As she was setting the last pie before the window to cool, Caroline came in from the yard.

The bucket sat on the corner of the deal table, and Caroline climbed on a rung of a nearby chair to get to it. Her short, plump arms reached over the edge of the bucket and pulled it close to the edge of the table. Plunging the gourd dipper into the full bucket, she lifted the water to her lips.

Cassie saw the bucket totter and sprang to the rescue, but not in time. Even as her hands reached for it, it crashed to the floor. Caroline stumbled from the chair rung and stood in the spreading water, her mouth and eyes wide in surprise and fear, the dipper still in her little hand.

Cassie's voice rose in rage. "Caroline, Caroline, see what thee has done! Thee is a wicked girl!"

Cassie grasped the handmade corn broom and swept the water out the door, barely missing John, who had come running to see what new excitement was afoot.

The water was gone, even the dipperful Caroline had had in her hand. Startled at her mother's angry words, she had dropped it too in the pool on the floor.

Never really fearful of Cassie in spite of her impatience, soon both of them were begging for water. Cassie said firmly, "You will both wait until evening for water, since your father brought none in and Caroline wickedly spilled what your mother carried. You will just have to wait. And you had better not stand there and cry, or I will bring in a switch from the peach tree. You would not want that."

John fearfully asked to go and get a bucket of water, but Cassie refused to allow it. He went out mournfully to play under the tree, but Caroline stood in the door, wailing over and over again, "I want a drink, Mother. I'm thirsty."

Cassie said sharply, "All right, Caroline, thee has asked for this and thee shall have it."

Cassie stepped out to the tree and broke a switch, stripping the leaves until only two remained. She switched Caroline until there were little red stripes on her bare legs, though, like Cassie, her skin was very white and it took but little to make such stripes.

John came to sit beside Caroline, and Cassie, seeing sympathy in his face, told him angrily that he, too, should sit there until his father came for supper.

Elias wakened and cried. Cassie knew that he, also, was thirsty, so she gave him her breast in place of the water she did not have. Then she put him on a pallet on the still damp floor.

It was thus that Ike found them when he came in wearily from the field. Seeing their tear-stained faces, he asked, "What is wrong with you?"

Cassie did not go to greet Ike, and the children explained to him in quavering voices. Though the milking was yet to be done, he took the water buckets and set off down the dusty road, taking John and Caroline with him. This would slow his trip, but Cassie knew that he wished to get them from under her feet.

When they returned, the children were no longer thirsty and seemed to have forgotten their troubles of the afternoon. Lizzie had given them freshly baked cookies, and both had saved a bite for their mother.

Ike brought the buckets in and set them down on the table. He said regretfully, "I am sorry, Cassie, that thee should have had such trouble because I forgot to carry the water at noon."

Cassie felt her old rush of love for Ike and was ready to forgive him, when her eye and his fell on the stack of broken dishes. Anger rose in her again, and she could not reply. Ike got the milk bucket and went to do the milking while Cassie finished preparing supper.

Even more tired than she had been all day, Cassie could not bring herself to scatter the clouds around the little table. Now there was not a blanket of love, but of anger.

Cassie thought that this time Ike should really be made to see what it meant not to have a well. She perhaps was too quick to forgive his neglect, or they would have had one long since!

Scarcely speaking, Cassie washed the supper dishes and prepared the children for bed. As she looked at them in their long white gowns, she held them close for a moment, then kissed them tenderly.

Cassie herself got ready for bed and, without looking at Ike, climbed into bed and turned her back to him, refusing to acknowledge the pleading in his eyes. As he crawled in beside her on the straw-filled tick, he put a gentle hand on her arm. She said a cold "Good night to thee, Ike" and turned firmly away from him.

"Cassie."

"What does thee want, Ike?"

"I will dig thy well for thee as soon as the threshers are gone."

Quickly she sat up in bed and looked down at him. "Will thee truly, Ike?"

"If the weather allows, I will, Cassie."

"I have no doubt thee hopes it will rain."

"Cassie, I promise thee I will dig thy well in spite of the rain."

Now Cassie returned the clasp of Ike's hand and kissed him good night, as was her usual custom, trying to ignore the voice inside her that said she had been wicked to Ike and to her children.

But Cassie could not help a great feeling of thankfulness that at last she was to have a well. Ike might not have kept a promise to do it as soon as he found the time, but this was definite. A Friend's promise was better than another man's oath. Ike would dig the well now, she knew.

The next day the work went quickly. The neighbor women came, and Cassie took pleasure in setting out the good food and feeding the hungry men. She would not think of her actions of the day before nor let this day be spoiled by remorse.

At last the threshing was over. That very evening Ike broke a V-shaped peach branch and went to find the spot for the well. As he carried it over the area in which he hoped to find water, he held one limb in each hand, the joint tilted up. At first the branch was motionless. Ike walked a few feet forward, and as Cassie watched, the branch began to turn in his hand until it pointed directly down. Then it was still, and Ike knew that there they would find water.

Cassie said admiringly, "Thee has a great gift, Ike."

Ike turned to her and smiled. Cassie knew that he felt this was a God-given power. Though he would go for miles around to find water for the neighbors, he did not like the words they used: "Ike Evans can witch a well."

⫸(XXI)⫷

Cassie went to bed that night happy in the knowledge that tomorrow they would begin the digging of the well. Enos Elliott had promised Ike that he would help him; this would be at some sacrifice, for there was yet much farm work to be done. Cassie felt again a prick of shame, but still she could not tell Ike she was sorry for the things she had said and done.

164

During the night, Cassie was awakened by thunder and a heat that was oppressive and threatening. The lightning flashed across the sky, and she drew close to Ike for comfort. She listened, but the children did not wake. Then the rain fell. Cassie felt a great foreboding. This did not seem like weather in which Ike could dig her a well.

Ike answered her doubt. "Thee need not fear, Cassie. I will dig at thy well tomorrow."

Again Cassie was ashamed and knew that she should tell Ike he must not dig if it would not be a good time. But she must have that well!

The rain had stopped by morning. As soon as the chores were done, Enos came, and they made a windlass with a rope and bucket. Thus, they could fill the bucket and pull it up when the hole was too deep for them to throw soil out with a shovel. They took turns with the digging. The rain of the night before and the sandiness of the soil made the digging easy.

Cassie could scarcely stay away from the work. Once she left the dishes uncleared on the table and went out to watch them. Ike handed her the shovel and said, "Here, Cassie, thee can take out a little thyself. Then thee can really believe it."

The digging went so fast that soon the well was ready for the lining of rocks. There would be plenty of water in the well—good water, like that they carried from the Elliotts'.

Ike told Enos that he should go back to his own tasks and leave the remaining work for him. Cassie saw Ike glance often at the cloudy sky, and she knew that a heavy rain would make it dangerous for him to go into the well. Yet the rocks must be put in place before the rain caused the sides to crumble.

Cassie, too, watched the skies, thinking that she should tell Ike to leave the work until it was safer. Indeed, Father had stopped and warned her that she must see that Ike was careful. Yet Father himself had felt she should see that Ike dug her a

165

well. And now that the well was finally being dug, she could not say the words that would make Ike delay. Ike was a careful person; he would not do anything he should not do.

That night Cassie again heard the rain. She thought of the long road to get water when the weather was hot. She would not let herself remember how she had resisted Ike's tenderness until he had given her his promise. After all, Ike realized it was her nature to be impatient. He knew that she loved him dearly and would never have said those things if she had not been over-tired. Ike would consider all this; she need not suggest that he stop until the danger was past. If Ike felt that he should stop, he would—or so Cassie told herself.

At last she slept, but fitfully, dreaming that Ike and Caroline and John were all at the bottom of a great hole while she and Elias stood looking at them. Elias was throwing little rocks down upon them. When Cassie wakened the next morning, she did not tell Ike of her dream.

As soon as the chores were done, Ike hurried to get to the work. The rain had stopped, but he went up and down carefully with the rocks. Cassie's work was neglected while she watched and helped as much as she could. When she had to work in the house or stay with the baby, she sent John to watch.

All day Ike worked, with only time off to eat and to do the chores that must be done. Even after supper he hurried out to do what he could before dark. It was on the tip of Cassie's tongue to say, "Let it go until morning, Ike. Thee knows thee should not work so late." But some evil spirit seemed to hold her tongue.

Ike looked so tired, so worn, that Cassie's feeling of guilt grew as she put the children to bed. For a moment she stood quietly looking down at them. Then, outside the window, she heard Ike's voice calling, "Cassie, Cassie."

She hurried to the window and looked out, but she could not see Ike. Again the voice came, "Cassie, Cassie."

She answered, "Yes, Ike, what is it?"

Still Cassie could not see him, but the voice was as clear as if he stood there by the house.

Cassie rushed outside, but Ike was not to be seen. It was his voice, but he was not there. She ran wildly, desperately, to the well. This had been no imagined voice, but a message of warning.

Going as close to the edge of the well as seemed safe, Cassie leaned far over and saw in awful terror that the side across from her had crumbled. Careful not to start this side falling, she cried, "Ike, Ike, where is thee? Where is thee?"

Praying that he might have gone to the barn, might be safe somewhere and not underneath the great pile of sand, Cassie knew that such hopes were vain. As surely as she had forced him to do something against his better judgment, he was down in the well, covered with sand.

As she looked, the sand, now within twenty feet of the top, moved. Ike must be under it.

The rope they had used in the windlass was there, and Cassie did not hesitate. Grasping it, she stepped over the edge, careful not to start another load of sand falling on top of Ike.

She did not stop to think what the rope would do to her hands. As she began to descend more quickly, she felt it burn her fingers. She thought how she might have cushioned her hands with her apron, but now she could not stop if she would.

When she reached the sand, she started to dig furiously with her raw hands, hardly feeling the burning pain. The sand was wet and heavy, and she prayed that she might, before it was too late, uncover enough of Ike for him to breathe. Surely God would not have sent her Ike's voice if it were already too late.

She saw no sign of life as she dug. A pile of sand grew behind her, and her fingers burned until the tears came to her eyes. Cassie did not think of her wickedness in driving Ike to this, but only of her love for him and of how she would not wish to live if she did not have Ike beside her.

She would not be good at bringing up her children without a father, Cassie thought. Ike had said that it was she who made their home so gay and happy, but surely it was Ike who made it safe and strong. She must not lose him, must not deprive her children of such a father.

And then, as she began to believe that it must surely be too late, Cassie felt his head with her burning fingers. She dug wildly, knowing now where to dig. Quickly she uncovered Ike's head, and with her hands and her skirts, she wiped his eyes and nose. He breathed! She could hear him breathe! And Cassie realized that it could not have been the hours it seemed since first she knew that he was covered.

Ike opened his sand-rimmed eyes and gasped, "Cassie."

Still digging, she tried to free his arms, saying only, "Thee must be still and rest, Ike."

But there was too much sand in the hole; it slipped back as fast as she dug it away. She must leave Ike, must somehow get up the rope and send John for help. She dared not go herself, for she must stay close to see that he was not covered again.

After a few minutes, Ike spoke feebly and directed her how best to climb the crumbling side. Cassie struggled up the rope, biting her lips to keep from crying out with pain as her raw hands rubbed against the coarse hemp. Once the earth gave way under her foot, and she hung for a moment ten feet above Ike's head. Cassie, agonized, held on to the rope, knowing all too well what it would mean if she fell on Ike. At last she found a firmer toehold and again started upward.

Almost to the top, she saw the sand give way and another

great avalanche go down. The sand was within an inch of Ike's mouth. Should she start John on his way or go back and clear the sand from Ike's head?

A new crumbling of the wall answered her question. The sand had reached Ike's mouth. This time covering her hands with her apron and clenching her teeth, she went down the rope.

Cassie cleared away the sand and, suddenly inspired with an idea, took off her shoes and stockings so that she would be less likely to disturb the sand. With her bare feet to aid her, she was soon at the top of the well. She looked down into the dimness, and it seemed to her that Ike's disembodied head was there on the bottom of the well. She shuddered with fear and began to run.

Reaching the house, Cassie pushed hard against the door, which was swollen and stuck from the rain. It suddenly gave way, and she was pitched to the floor inside. She jumped up and flew into the room where John slept beside his sister.

"John, John," she whispered. "Thee must wake and help thy mother!"

It was good that John could waken and have possession of his faculties in a moment, was steady and strong, so that she could depend on him when she so needed him. Quickly she explained to him what he must do and helped him put on his pants. Cassie lighted the lantern and told him to hurry for Enos. She could see the fear in his eyes. Perhaps he remembered that, even yet, there were Indians who passed this way.

She said, "Take Nick with thee. Thee need not fear, John. God will care for thee. Thy father and I will pray while thee goes. All will be well. Thee is a man to do this for thy parents."

As Cassie helped John out the door, she wondered how she could ever have been cross with him, with Caroline, and with Ike. If God spared them Ike, she would never again be as she had been this last week. Then Cassie added that, whether God spared or took Ike, she would never again act so, for she knew man could not bargain with God.

Cassie hurried back to the well and down the rope, unable now to see even the white blur of Ike's face. When she reached him, he was weak and tired, but still able to speak.

Crouching beside him, Cassie placed her cheek against his and poured out all her sorrow, all her penitence for the things she had done and said, and told him of the voice that had saved him. And then she prayed that God would care for John.

As she finished, Ike replied weakly, "Amen."

Cassie said tenderly, "Thee knows how sorry I am—that I will never scold thee so again, doesn't thee, Ike?"

Ike smiled with his parched lips. His weak but loving voice answered, "Thee will, Cassie. Thee should. The Lord sent thee to me, thee knows. And Solomon says, 'The words of the wise are as goads.' Thee knows, Cassie, I sometimes need a goad."

Cassie's smile was a little twisted. "I never wished to be a goad to thee, Ike."

"I did not say thee was a goad, only that thy words were wise."

Cassie leaned over and kissed him there in the dimness. "Thee must be quiet and rest, Ike, until help arrives."

So it had come to this. Cassie, who wished only to bring joy and happiness to Ike, had become a goad. And there was an even less happy thought: she had withheld her love until Ike had promised to do as she wished. Cassie knew what kind of woman must have pay for her love.

It should not be Ike who must suffer for Cassie's wickedness, perhaps pay with his very life. Who could say how such an experience might affect him? Even if help did arrive in time to get him out, he might well be a sick man.

Cassie knew she should pray for Ike, not worry about her own wrongdoing. Calmer now, she thought only of Ike's welfare and of her love for him. She said prayers for Ike's well-being and prayers of thankfulness for what God had already done for them.

As Cassie sat beside Ike, there came to her a great peace, the peace that passeth all understanding. The presence of God and His sheltering care seemed all around them.

Then she heard the sound of Enos's horse bringing him to their rescue. She thanked God again and said, "Hear, Ike; he is coming! Enos will soon be here."

A light shone above the well and Enos called, "Cassie, Cassie!"

"We are here, Enos."

"How is thee? Is Ike—?"

"Yes, God has been good."

As they spoke, Enos was already preparing to send down the lantern, saying, "When thee comes up, I will go down and help bring up the sand, and so we can get Ike out. Lizzie has gone for Ike's brothers. Put the rope under thy arms."

With Enos to help, it was easier. Now with the windlass working, they soon had Ike so that he could breathe more freely. Ike said weakly that there were needles in his arms and legs.

It seemed a long time before they heard the horses of Wesley and also of Samuel, who had been summoned by Lizzie as though there were no ill will between him and Ike. Little things were forgotten in such a calamity.

They lifted Ike out, bruised and sore, but alive. Carrying him gently, they laid him on the bed. Cassie said they must call the doctor, but Ike replied, "No, I need no doctor, just rest."

When Lizzie saw Cassie's torn and bleeding hands, she

bound them with ointment in strips of worn sheeting. Lizzie would stay through the night to help with the work until Mother Ballinger could be brought.

Enos said as he went out the door, "Thee shall yet have thy well, Cassie. We will all come, Ike's brothers, both of them, and place the rock for thee after we take out the sand that covered Ike."

Thinking that Ike at least would understand her words, Cassie replied, "Thank thee, Enos, and the Lord bless thee. But I would not goad thee to this task. It is more than I deserve that thee should be so good to me."

Enos's tone was kind. "Thee is young, Cassie. Thee has waited patiently, and as thee gets older thee will find even more patience. Now we will go and tell John he has saved his father's life. He can stay the day with our children."

Her voice was unsteady. "Tell John that his mother says he has been a man this night."

Cassie had never known such thankfulness. From the strain and the grief, she felt a kind of lightness, almost as if she were in a dream. At last she slept beside Ike and wakened to find her mother there to care for them.

⌒⟨ XXII ⟩⌒

IF IKE HAD THE SEWING MACHINE TO REMIND HIM OF HIS BEHAVior toward Cassie, surely Cassie would never drink water from her well without being reminded of how far she had fallen short of the glory of God. She had learned, but so slowly! Cassie could not look at her well with any joy, nor forget the sorrow she had brought upon them.

Finally Ike said, "Cassie, thee is being very foolish. Thee

should not blame thyself so. If I had dug thy well long ago, or had let thy father give it to thee as might have been right, this need not have happened. It is my pride that has caused this thing.

"Thee told me," he continued, "to forget as thee would what I had done. Now thee, too, must forget and enjoy thy well as thee does thy sewing machine. When we are old, it will not matter one way or the other. Let us enjoy our youth and be gay."

Cassie felt a great surge of joy; now it was Ike who wished to be gay. So they put behind them the things that had happened and found life good again.

Then a letter came to Ike from Mother Evans. She wrote, "Thy father seems a bit feeble to me. Can thee not bring thy family and come to thy old home for a while?"

Cassie said quickly, "No, Ike, thee knows we cannot all go. But thee must go. It is a season when we can get on without thee. John is a big boy, and the fall work is done."

Cassie saw that Ike did indeed wish to see his father, if his conscience would allow him to leave them there alone. So she pressed him to go and said that Father would be glad to drop over every few days and see that all was well. Thomas and Esther also promised to help Cassie. And since Enos Elliott's cow was now dry, he would be glad to do their milking for a part of the milk. Both Father and Enos told Ike to go and not to worry about his family.

At last it was decided that he would go for two weeks, and Father took Ike to the train. As Cassie saw them go out of sight, she began to realize what it was to be lonely. Not since they had been married had she been separated from him. How could she be lonely with three busy children? Yet, when her thoughts had circled around her husband for so long, it was hard to be without him.

It was difficult for Cassie to cook without the thought of Ike's joy in the food. The evenings seemed long, and the children no company at all to her. It did seem queer that life could be like that. What if she did not know that Ike would soon be back? Then, in spite of her children, life would seem very empty.

Cassie occupied herself with her tasks, and she and the children began to count the days until Ike would return. Elias had now begun to play actively with his brother and sister. Cassie thought that Ike would scarcely know his son when he returned from his long visit.

There were letters saying that Father Evans had failed greatly but that he was enjoying this time with Ike. He had wanted to see Cassie and his grandchildren, but he could understand that they were unable to leave.

Ike was with his parents for Thanksgiving, and Cassie and the children went to spend the night with Father and Mother Ballinger. This made them all happier than staying at home and missing Ike.

Cassie had known that Ike was her very life, but she had not known how it would be to have him gone. They would show him when he returned how they had missed him. Cassie thought sometimes that if Ike missed them as much as they did him, perhaps he would not stay the full two weeks. Father Evans must need him sorely, or Ike could not stay.

At last the two weeks were over, and Father drove into the yard with Ike. He did not even get down from the wagon but left at once, saying, "Thee will want this time with thy family." Dear Father, he could be a very understanding man.

Supper was ready when Ike arrived, but it was long before they could sit down to eat. The children swarmed around Ike, asking him questions, exclaiming over the little gifts he had brought them, vying with each other to see who could sit on his lap.

Cassie felt her world right itself again as she stood watching them. When they sat down to dinner, she was moved to give thanks for Ike's safe return and for the joy of being together again.

After the children had been put to bed, Ike said, "Father is not likely to be with us long, Cassie. I wish thee could have gone since thee loves Father, and he thee, from the visit we made when first we were married. But he sees that thee could not come. And it would not have been good for him to have our noisy family to worry him."

So it was that, even in the midst of joy, there was pain. But Father Evans was old, older than Cassie's parents by many years, and Ike was the youngest of his children.

Except for their worry about Father Evans, and the bad news which came of him, Christmas and New Year's were joyous times. The days seemed to pass more swiftly, and the children were no longer babies. Even Elias, now a year old, was beginning to walk around holding to the chairs.

Then Cassie knew there would be yet another baby and was glad. If it should be a boy, they would name it David for Father Evans, hoping it would be as good and gentle a soul as he.

With the well and the sewing machine, with John now old enough to save her steps, Cassie had her work well in hand. Her spirit was more controlled, too. She had learned the folly of getting her values mixed, of thinking it important that her husband's relatives should find her skilled in sewing.

It came to Cassie over and over that only loving God and one's fellow man were really important. And sometimes she thought she knew what Friends meant by the Inner Light. She would never forget that she had heard Ike's voice and so had been able to help save his life. But that was not all. There were times when she seemed to feel the very presence of God as she knew Mother so often did.

She said to Ike, "Does thee see, Ike, that thy wife has become very settled and a little old these days?"

He looked at her with his slow smile and said, "Thee looks very young and not at all settled to me, Cassie. I hope thee does not make a gay man out of thy husband and then become mournful and staid thyself."

As Ike was getting ready for his spring work, a letter came from Mother Evans, saying that, if Ike wished to see his father alive, he must come.

With Samuel and Wesley, Ike reached his home a day before his father died. Mother Ballinger came to stay with the children, and Father Ballinger went with Cassie to the funeral. As Cassie looked at Father Evans, it seemed that even in death there was a kind of light about his face, and in it Cassie could see much of Ike.

Several days later they returned home. Mother Evans would stay on her farm as long as she could. One of the grandchildren who lived nearby would farm it and move in with her. Cassie thought sadly that this could not last. She had seen the grandson's wife and felt that she was not a young woman who would long abide Mother Evans's ways.

The summer passed quickly, with Ike busier because of the delay. Almost before it seemed possible, Ninth Month arrived and, with it, little David. This time Mother did not stay with Cassie, since one of Enos Elliott's daughters was old enough to come and help until school started.

Cassie found her new serenity a help with her added work. She was careful not to allow John to take too much responsibility, though it was hard to restrain him since he was so willing. She did not want him to be like Ike, a young man old before his time. She tried to develop in him a spirit of gaiety, not an easy task in so sober a child.

Ike told her with a tender smile, "Thee need not worry about John, Cassie. With so much love in his home, thee need not fear that he will be unhappy. Thee knows that I am very happy, that thee has made me so, but thee sees, too, that I do not laugh as readily as thee does. That is no sign that I am not now gay on the inside."

Cassie saw that she must show John, perhaps even more than the others, her great love for him. Yet she must be careful that Caroline, who was indeed gay, should not be hurt or jealous for any reason. Sometimes Caroline became naughty when it seemed that John was singled out for praise.

With each day there were new matters to solve. It must be very hard for people who had no Inner Light to guide them when life became so complex.

Rachel and Wesley came to spend the day during corn shocking. While Wesley and Ike were working in the field, Rachel spoke of Mother Evans, who was unhappy with her grandson's wife, Abigail. She was, it seemed, a young woman with a mind of her own and would not bend to Mother Evans's will.

Cassie noted that Rachel was unwilling to think of what might happen should this arrangement fail entirely. In wonder she heard Rachel speak of their "crowded household." Cassie did not ask how they could be crowded with such a large house and with their two older children about to be married and in homes of their own.

Cassie would not hurry the trouble she feared. No doubt it would come without invitation. So she did not answer Rachel with any words or opinions of her own.

177

Always after talking with his brothers Ike seemed concerned, and Cassie would see him sitting in silent thought. She resolved that she would wait for Ike to bring up the problem himself. Cassie knew that she could not say nay if Ike asked her to allow Mother Evans to come and live with them.

Cassie resolved that her family must enjoy this lovely autumn while they could. This year Ike had planted popcorn, and they hung it to dry in the woodshed where the mice could not reach it. The children brought in walnuts, and John's hands were black for weeks from hulling them. Cassie looked at the red leaves on the trees and tried to think only of the beauty of the earth, to put away the foreboding she felt when she allowed the thought of Mother Evans to enter her mind.

Then a letter came, a letter addressed as always to Ike alone, written in the old-fashioned script which seemed to Cassie like Mother Evans herself: firm and unyielding, yet somehow cramped and unhappy. Ike did not open it at first, but evidently wished to wait as long as possible before knowing its message. At last he opened the letter slowly and read it, but he still did not say what it contained. When the children had gone out to play, he said, "Things are not working out with Mother and Abigail."

"I know. Rachel told me," Cassie replied.

He went on soberly. "Wesley says that Rachel says there is no room for her there, and Samuel himself says there is not room in his home. Mother could go to my sister's close to her home there, but it seems right that it should be a son who would provide a home for his mother, not a son-in-law. So it must be between the three of us here. What does thee think, Cassie?"

Cassie thought that this might be a good time to begin counting before she spoke, as Father had told her to do long ago. She would no doubt be doing much of that if Mother Evans came.

Yet, because she loved Ike and could not hurt him, she would not deny him.

But Cassie could not help asking, "Does thee want her to come, Ike?"

"She is old, Cassie. Thee must know it would be cruel to be in thy old age and have no one want thee."

Ike had chosen the best way to appeal to Cassie, who could not bear for anyone to feel unloved or unwanted.

So she said, "We will share our home and our love with her, Ike, if thee wishes." Then solemnly, "I will try very hard to get along with thy mother. But thee will remember that already she does not think me the wife for thee. Thee must help me with this."

Ike's face was so relieved, so nearly happy, that Cassie felt repaid for her acceptance of what she knew would be hard for all of them. If only Ike would not allow his mother to force him back into the old mold of sobriety, if only he would not feel again that it was somehow wrong to be gay and light-hearted!

⊰ XXIII ⊱

IKE WOULD SOON RETURN WITH MOTHER EVANS AND HER TRUNK in the spring wagon. Cassie spoke quickly. "John, Caroline, you must not smear the glass with your noses. Your father and grandmother will soon be here. You know we must have everything neat for your grandmother."

Cassie took a last look around the room, this time through Mother Evans's eyes. Then with the proud eyes of a mother, she viewed the two children eagerly watching from the window, Elias playing on the floor, and David sleeping in his cradle. Cassie thought that she herself would prefer to see the round smudges on the pane that bespoke an eager welcome.

She had little doubt that Mother Evans would love and approve seven-year-old John, who was so like his father Ike.

But Caroline! Cassie knew already that Caroline's great likeness to her would be no recommendation to Ike's mother. The red, curly hair that made a little flame around her small face would not bespeak the plainness Mother Evans insisted they all should have.

Cassie had tried, though perhaps not hard enough, all through the years of her marriage to forget that first visit they had paid to Ike's home, to forget the words that had cut her so cruelly in her youth and inexperience when first Mother Evans had seen the redness and curliness of her hair and had said, "Thy hair is very bright. Did thee never think thee should cover it with a cap to hide it?"

Nor had Cassie forgotten that she had offended Mother Evans by a quick answer to another remark. She had so shamed Ike that even her apology to Mother Evans had not wiped out the memory for all of them.

Ike had not wanted her to wear a cap then. Would he now, with his mother a part of their home, with her disapproving eye always on the red hair which Cassie had passed on to Caroline and David?

And, as Caroline grew older, would her grandmother try to force her to wear a cap? As Cassie thought of this and of the difficulty of forcing Caroline to do anything, she knew that there would be trouble—trouble not just between Caroline and her grandmother, for she herself would join in, often on Caroline's side! Then, since Cassie was much opposed to the crossing of bridges before they were reached, she put this problem out of her mind. It would come soon enough.

She thought hopefully that Mother Evans had only to look

at this cheerful room and these happy, healthy children to see that all was well in her son's home. They would teach Mother Evans to be happy and loving, as they themselves were. Ike had lost much of his solemn mien; why not Mother Evans also? No doubt she had never been part of a merry home before.

Cassie set her chin firmly. She would conquer this feeling that she must say good-by to all the good years she had had in this room, to her place as the center of the little family that lived and loved here. Such foreboding would not aid in her resolve to make Ike's mother happy and contented, to curb her own impatient spirit, and to honor Ike's mother as Ike would wish, as Ike himself honored her mother.

As Cassie thought of Ike's great love for Mother Ballinger and of the pleasure they found in each other's company, she knew that that too would be likely to cause hard feelings.

The old visits they had all enjoyed so much—how could they continue with Ike's mother sitting like a warning conscience, her face disapproving, her eyes cold? A great flood of sadness for all the happy times now gone, which surely could never be again so long as Mother Evans was there, rushed over Cassie, and she felt hot tears in her eyes.

Caroline, unaware of the trouble about to come upon them— and no doubt most heavily upon her—called in a happy little squeal, "Mother, Mother, they are here! Does thee see? They are here."

Cassie stood behind the children and brought a smile to her lips, at the same time praying silently for grace. God had sent Ike's mother here, perhaps as a test for her, and He would help her meet her tribulations. If only, somehow, she could be constantly blessed with that Inner Light her own mother knew!

She watched Ike lift the bent figure from the spring wagon— a figure that seemed small to Cassie, shrunken since the last time she had seen her. Cassie's heart warmed to Mother Evans in compassion. This was the woman who had first loved Ike. How sad to be old and truly important to no one, first in the heart of no living person!

But would Ike ever again lift Cassie from the wagon and hold her high while she struggled a little in fun to delight the children? There would be no place for such foolishness under Mother Evans's watchful eye.

Cassie gave Caroline one last word of admonition. "Caroline, thee must not fret thy grandmother." Caroline's eyes were wide and guileless.

Cassie straightened a chair, placed Caroline's rag doll in the bed Ike had made for it, and opened the door in welcome.

Mother Evans walked with resolute briskness across the grass and up the steps to the porch. Cassie leaned over to kiss the dry cheek. With God's help, she said warmly, "Thee is welcome in our home, Mother Evans."

Behind his mother, Ike's naturally solemn face beamed. Cassie felt rewarded. She prayed that Ike had forgotten her first ungraciousness the morning the letter arrived, the letter written to Ike alone, though it was also Cassie's home to which Mother Evans must come.

His face was happy now. He was secure in Cassie's promise to do her best, perhaps hopeful that, as he had become more cheerful married to Cassie, it might be that some miracle could be worked with his mother. Cassie prayed again that she might be able to help with that miracle. It must indeed be a miracle to work such a change in Mother Evans.

Cassie opened the door to the parlor, which was her pride, the room she always had ready for guests, never cluttered by the children's play. It held the pieces that Mother Ballinger had brought from the East, pieces that she had passed on to Cassie when Father Ballinger had bought a new set of furniture. The new was in reality no better than the old. And Cassie secretly thought that Father realized Ike would accept discarded furniture although he would never allow Father to give them anything new.

"Here is thy room, Mother Evans."

Cassie made her voice warm with a welcome she must feel for Ike's sake. She threw wide the presses from which she had reluctantly removed her own things.

"Priscilla lent us a bed for thy room." Cassie could not help wondering why Samuel and Priscilla could not have allowed Mother Evans to occupy this same bed in their home. Her uncharitable feeling was that they had eased their consciences by the sacrifice of the bed.

Mother Evans looked about the room, then hung her cape in the closet without a word to show that she must see they had given her their best.

Suddenly the room no longer seemed warm and cheerful, the pretty room that Cassie had thought it was before. It was only a place where one could sleep, not live and be happy. They had built a fire in the fireplace, but there seemed a chill in the air. Cassie shivered and led the way back to the room where supper waited.

As they stepped into the kitchen, it seemed suddenly full of people—too small, much too small, for three generations. How could one person, and that person no longer tall and commanding but somehow shrunken, so completely fill a room? Ike had said, "Samuel's and Wesley's families are large. We have only four." Cassie had not reminded him that his brothers' houses were large, too.

Now her smile was tender as she caught his eye. Ike was sensitive where his ability to provide for his family was concerned. She would not speak to him of the smallness of their home.

The tenderness she felt for Ike spread to envelop Mother

Evans, who must surely in great measure be responsible for Ike's goodness.

The tenderness came out in the warmth of her words. "Thee must feel at home with us, Mother Evans."

Mother Evans, her voice carefully firm, answered this welcome. "Thank thee, Cassie. I will endeavor not to be in thy way."

"There will be no question of being in our way, Mother Evans. Thee will be one of us." Filled with sympathy for the old lady, who must surely be homesick for her own house and the things she had cared about for so many years, Cassie truly meant the words she said.

They seated themselves at the table filled with the best that Cassie could prepare. Cassie listened eagerly to Mother Evans's tale of her train trip; though always glad to be in her own home, Cassie found travel very exciting.

The children were full of questions, and Cassie smiled restrainingly at them, aware that in Mother Evans's home her children had been taught to be seen, not heard. Cassie herself had never had such training, so she had not taught it to her children.

Mother Evans seemed not to hear the children's questions and finished her tale by saying, "A tiring trip, my son."

Were all her remarks to be for Ike only, even as her letters, which had always closed, "To my son Isaac, from his Mother." There had never even been regards to his children and to Cassie.

Cassie remembered how eagerly the children had greeted their grandmother this evening and how indifferent she had seemed. Surely there was none of the pleasure Cassie believed a grandmother would feel when first she saw the four children of her youngest son.

With supper over, Cassie made her words sincere and kind.

"Thee must lie down since thee has finished thy meal, Mother Evans. Thee must rest from thy trip for a while; then we will visit before the fire."

"I did not come to be a burden to thee, Cassie." Mother Evans's tone was stern, but Cassie saw underneath it the loneliness and the determination not to be dependent. "Lie down indeed! I will wash the dishes while thee works at thy sewing." Did her eyes go to the buttonhole on Ike's coat hanging from the nail beside the door? Did Cassie only imagine that there was disapproval in Mother Evans's glance at the sewing machine Cassie prized so highly? No doubt Ike's mother would believe it willful extravagance to have such a timesaver. Cassie thought with a little smile to herself that they had paid for the machine with great sacrifice.

Indeed, Ike had suggested that his mother could be a help to her. He had said, "Thee has so much work to do, Cassie, even though thee has only four children." And another time, "My mother is noted for her fine sewing and her tailoring. She can teach thee if thee wishes. Though thee knows I am well satisfied with thee."

Cassie sighed. Surely, by this time, one should be more skillful. She put a sheltering hand over the buttonhole at her own throat.

Where was the satisfaction she had begun to feel in her sewing since she had gotten the machine? If one glance from Mother Evans—and that possibly only imagined—could shatter her confidence, she should allow herself to be taught, she should conquer her wicked pride and *ask* Mother Evans to teach her. Cassie resolved that she would defeat this folly in herself.

"Perhaps thee would be willing to make some buttonholes later in the week when thee is rested. I am not good at them, and Ike tells me thee is noted for thy sewing."

185

"Thee will not learn if thee does not work at it. I will show thee, and thee can practice."

Cassie set her teeth firmly. It was one thing to ask someone to teach; it was quite another to have someone insist on teaching. But this was Ike's mother. And the time at the very beginning of her stay was important.

Yet surely the Lord did not will that she should turn over the reins of her home to such a righteous old lady, even if she were Ike's mother. Indeed, it might be important in another way, this time when they began their life together.

"As thee wishes about the sewing," Cassie replied. "But I will wash my dishes."

Mother Evans stood at her elbow as she worked, more than merely willing to help. At last Cassie handed her a cloth for drying. They finished the task in silence.

Caroline came running to her grandmother, her first shyness gone. "Grandmother, will thee make my doll a dress?"

"Indeed not, Caroline. I am sure thy mother has more important tasks for me to do."

Cassie said slowly, even patiently, "To Caroline, a dress for her doll is important. I will make thee one tomorrow, Caroline."

"Is thee not teaching her the wickedness of idle tasks, Cassie? Surely thee does not wish to foster worldliness in thy child!"

Ah, yes, Cassie had always known that Ike's mother thought her worldly. Though Friends did not gossip, Cassie had no doubt that Ike's brothers' wives had told Mother Evans of Cassie's father, who had more than once been called before the meeting. And Cassie had not forgotten that Mother Evans had found the French blood, of which both Father and Cassie were proud, something of which they might well be ashamed.

Carefully, not allowing her indignation to show in her tone, she answered the accusation. "I do not consider the learning of motherhood an idle or a worldly task. Caroline feels a motherliness for her doll."

The older woman's lips pressed firmly and righteously together.

Cassie added quickly, "Let there be no contention between us, Mother Evans. Thee knows we wish thee to be happy with us."

"It is not important that I be happy, only that we tread in the narrow path of godliness."

"But surely thee sees that God placed the flowers along the path to be enjoyed."

Mother Evans's lips quivered, and Cassie pressed her advantage. "We cannot all see eye to eye on little things, Mother Evans. Let us not make small matters grow large."

"This is *thy* home, Cassie."

After they had gone to bed, Cassie asked herself how, on the first evening of Mother Evans's life with them, things could have gone so badly. She was glad that Ike had been busy putting the children to bed, a task with which he often helped her, and had not heard the words that passed between her and his mother.

The days went by with none of the bounding joy Cassie was wont to find in them.

Each morning Cassie tried to influence Mother Evans to lie in bed until the house was warm, since it was not needful that she rise to help with breakfast. Her answers were always short. "I will do my duty to thee, Cassie." Like Ike, she could not bear to be "beholden" to anyone.

One day Mother Evans did not rise as early as usual, and Ike was in from the milking before she came out of her room. Glad of the few minutes alone with Ike, Cassie stooped over him as he waited at the table and kissed him gaily on his nose. He put a long arm around her and pulled her to him.

As they were thus, Mother Evans's door opened and she stood in the entrance, taking in the scene, which had been such a usual one before her coming.

Mother Evans said nothing, but her expression was telling.

Cassie felt herself pulling away from the arm Ike had already dropped. She saw something like shame on Ike's face as he greeted his mother. A rush of warmth flooded Cassie's cheeks—not embarrassment, but anger that Ike should feel so and that she herself should allow his mother's disapproval to shame her in any way.

After this, it seemed that all of Cassie's teaching of love and gaiety had been for naught. The demonstrations of affection which had at last seemed natural to Ike were now secret snatches that left Cassie ashamed and Ike uncomfortable, again a little boy, anxious for his mother's approval.

Ike had become almost as Cassie had hoped that he *could* become with her and with the children, almost as freely loving as Father Ballinger, though still without his gaiety. Now it was all undone. He seemed to be a different person from the Ike she knew. Reserved as when first she knew him, Ike now had a look that seemed to her almost as disapproving as his mother's. Even at night when they retired from his mother's presence, he seemed somehow ashamed of his love. His embraces were quick, as though, as Peter wrote, he "warred in his members."

Cassie shrank from him as she had never thought to do, unable to believe that such a thing could have happened to them. In all her foreboding she had not thought of this.

This, then, was that of which the Bible spoke and called it *Lust*. This was no part of the love they had had, no part of their joyous marriage.

↽ XXIV ↾

IN SPITE OF HER RESOLVE NOT TO BOW TO MOTHER EVANS'S RULE, Cassie saw them all, even herself, walking a narrow plank, catering to Ike's mother's prejudices, spoken and unspoken.

Cassie grew to know every downward-curving line of Mother Evans's countenance. John, always sober, was now almost mournful. Caroline's dancing spirit, so oft restrained, came out in naughtiness. Cassie found herself comforting Caroline and standing out against Mother Evans, sometimes in secret, in a way she herself hated.

"Idle words, idle words!" was her grandmother's reply to Caroline's flights of fancy and fun. Whereas Mother Evans would not have spoken to Cassie in reproach for her actions, she felt free to speak as she wished to a child.

Cassie looked in the tiny mirror and saw her mouth becoming grim from constant self-discipline. Did God really disapprove of happiness and joy? Was sorrow really better than laughter, and was the heart made better by the sadness of the countenance? Must little children forget how to smile?

Surely Cassie had known better times.

Cassie had to admit, however, that Mother Evans was of great help to her with her work. No longer was the mending basket full. The clothes she made on her sewing machine were perfectly finished by Mother Evans's gnarled, old fingers. And no longer did Ike's buttonholes resemble the eyes of the pigs he fed each morning and evening.

Sometimes Cassie was surprised to see a tenderness on the old lady's face as the children begged for fresh-baked cookies. Mother Evans would give them some, but always as though she were ashamed of her weakness. Cassie wondered what penance Ike's mother did that simple joys could seem so wrong to her.

Morning and night Cassie prayed for strength and patience so that she might not hurt Ike by striving with his mother. She told herself that she had made some headway, though now it seemed that the hurt his mother had caused went deeper than any surface contention. She seemed sometimes to have undermined the whole foundation of their lives.

One night after one of Ike's almost furtive embraces, Cassie said painfully, "Ike, does thee not see that something has happened to our home? Does thee think I am unkind to thy mother?"

"What does thee mean, Cassie? Of course it must be different with an older person here. But I see only kindness from thee to my mother. She is not a gay person, but I was not so gay until I found thee."

Cassie knew she should be glad that Ike did not feel the rancor she herself felt. Oh, but it was more than rancor.

The next evening Ike came in from his work and said, "Cassie, thy mother expects us this evening. We have not seen thy parents for a month now—not since Mother came to be with us."

Cassie stared at Ike. When had he seen her mother? She had not known he had left the farm. He turned to Mother Evans. "Would thee stay with the children while we go to Cassie's parents' home?"

"If thee wishes, Ike."

After supper was over and the dishes done, Ike brought the horse to the block, and they set out in the crisp night, Cassie behind Ike with her arms around him.

"Ike, when did thee see Mother?" She asked. "How did thee know she wished to see us?"

"Cassie, thy mother always wishes to see us."

"I know, Ike, but thee said she expects us. How did thee know?"

"Thy mother and I are very close. I know she expects us."

Cassie was humbled. "Oh, Ike, thee has had a revelation! Why did thee not tell me? But thee is so good it does not seem strange to me. Thee is quiet and listens. Like Mother." She sighed. "Mother says Father and I do not wait on the Lord."

"It is only since I have known thy mother that this has come to me," Ike said gently.

"I have always known my mother, but only the time when thee was covered in the well did I have a revelation. Why can I not be still and listen?"

"Cassie, do not fret." Ike's voice was tender. "Thee is so good. Thee, too, will have this joy when it is time."

"I hope so, Ike. But I know I am an impatient person."

"Thee shows great patience with my mother, Cassie. Because I cannot speak as freely as thee does, never think I do not see and appreciate."

Cassie could only wonder if he truly did see.

"Cassie, thy father and mother have not seen their grandchildren for weeks now. Why do we not ask them for dinner soon? And we can also invite Esther and Thomas. After all, Esther is Mother's granddaughter. Would it be too hard for thee to have so many?"

"Oh, Ike, that will be good!" Cassie answered with rising excitement. "But will thy mother wish to see Esther, since she is out of the meeting and Samuel and Priscilla will not see her?"

"Cassie, thee must not allow Mother's attitudes to deter thee. It is our home, and Esther and Thomas are our friends."

Cassie was astonished. Did Ike not see that his mother's attitudes now shaped them all, even when she was not in the room with them? Could Ike not see that even the children were now different?

She would talk to Mother about this. She would not consult Father, for he would see only Cassie's side, and no one needed to point that side out to her.

As they rode up to the block, Father came bustling out. "Thy mother expected thee this evening," he said as he helped Cassie down and kissed her.

"Did *thee*, Father?" Cassie asked.

"Of course, Cassie. Thee knows I trust thy mother's insight."

Cassie sighed. "I know thee does. But why does thee not know these things without being told?"

Father answered, "Does thee think perhaps the Lord is satisfied with one in the family?"

"No, Father, and neither does thee. Mayhap thee and thy daughter do not listen as they should."

Mother met them at the door and greeted them as if they were both her own children—children who had been away too long.

After the news of the family had been told, Mother said to Cassie, "Thee must see the quilt I have in."

When they were in the big kitchen by the crackling fire, Mother said, "Cassie, thee has been troubled."

"Yes, Mother, sorely. Our home is changed now that Ike's mother has come."

"I know thee prays for wisdom and grace, Cassie. It can be very hard to have thy house so full. Does thee find no comfort when thee prays?"

"Some comfort, Mother." Cassie sighed. "But soon I am troubled again. Mother, does thee think I am frivolous, worldly?"

"Thee knows I do not, Cassie. Unwise, sometimes, and too quick to speak. But then thee knows we are not so sober as some of the Friends, as Ike's family. Ike—how does he feel about thy trouble with his mother?"

"I cannot tell him if he cannot see. She is his mother, and he loves her. My great concern is that he may become as sober as his family again. Ike said thee expected us this evening. If he can see such things, why can he not see the trouble in his home, the problems we have?"

"He is used to his mother. Does she speak harshly before Ike?"

"Mother, it is not so much what she says as how disapproving she looks. Our children are changed already. John is more sober. Caroline is rebellious, and Mother Evans finds her naughty. Thee knows she is like thy daughter. Did thee find me always naughty?"

"No, Cassie. Mischievous often, but I seldom found thee naughty. But thee knows we do not find the Friends' way a joyless discipline. Thee has been constantly in my prayers. The Lord will show thee a way if thee listens."

"Thy prayers seem more useful than mine. If Ike could see the need for prayers—"

Mother interrupted. "I am sure he does, Cassie. Ike's understanding is greater than thee thinks."

Cassie changed the subject, not wishing to dwell on it. "Ike wants thee and Father and Esther and Thomas to come to our house for dinner soon. Does thee think his mother will be upset to see Esther?"

"Cassie, thee must trust Ike more," Mother said firmly. "Thee feels he does not see his mother's attitude, and thee does not credit him with a wish to help thee. Be sure he is wise and is working for thy good and his family's, as well as his mother's. Thee shows a lack of faith. Of course we must accept this invitation, and Esther and Thomas must come."

Cassie put her cheek against her mother's. "If I could see thee more often, I might grow in faith. Was thee always so, Mother?"

"We grow in understanding, Cassie. Ike is not the same young man thee married. And thee, too, has changed."

"Not always for the better, I fear. When I had the revelation about the well, I thought I would begin to be like thee, so sure and serene."

"Oh, Cassie, I would not wish thee to be as I am. We are all different; God made us that way. But He does not send more than we can bear."

"Sometimes Ike's mother seems more than anyone could bear. Thee must hold me in thy prayers so that I may grow in patience."

They joined Father and Ike, who were making plans for the visit. Father would ride over and invite Thomas and Esther, who lived closer to the Ballingers. They would arrange for next Third Day, and, unless Father let them know at once, Cassie would prepare.

As she and Ike rode away, Cassie said, "I doubt thy mother will make Esther welcome when Samuel and Priscilla do not."

"Why, Cassie, it is for us to make Esther welcome in our home. Does thee think it is no longer thy home, that it should be my mother who should welcome our guests?"

Cassie was somewhat comforted. "Thee is right, Ike. I must not look for trouble."

They planned the visit. Cassie said, "We can feed the children first, so they will not be hungry and fretful." This seemed to meet Ike's approval, though Cassie knew that when there was company in Ike's mother's home, the children had waited until the elders had eaten.

By noon the next day Father had not come, so Ike told his mother the plan.

Her mouth set in its lines of disapproval. "Thee would still encourage Esther in her disobedience? Thy brother's wishes do not matter to thee, I see. Or thy mother's. Thee has forgotten thy early training, Ike."

Ike's tone was calm but sure. "Mother, we do what is the Lord's will. Our niece Esther and Thomas are always welcome in our home. And it is time thee met Cassie's mother and saw her father again. We look forward to a happy day with them."

Mother Evans did not answer, but Cassie could see no joyous anticipation on the white old face.

Now that Ike seemed aware of their problem, Cassie felt more hopeful and entered with joy into the preparation for the meal. Mother Evans helped, as she believed it to be her duty.

On the day of the dinner, Thomas and Esther came first. While Thomas put the horse away, Esther brought the baby into the kitchen, which was full of the odors of pumpkin pie and roasting chicken.

Cassie drew Esther forward to Mother Evans and said, "This is thy granddaughter and thy great-granddaughter, Mother Evans. Esther, thy grandmother."

For a moment, Cassie feared Ike's mother would not respond to her introduction. But there were sudden tears in the old eyes, and Esther quickly handed the baby to Cassie and took the worn hands in her own. "Grandmother, it is good to see thee. Father has spoken of thee so often."

Mother Evans, reminded of her son's disapproval, seemed about to voice her own when the door opened to Ike and Thomas. Ike said, "Mother, this is our good friend, Thomas Keith."

Mother Evans nodded coldly and continued peeling the potatoes, a chore that had been interrupted when Esther and her baby entered.

When Father and Mother Ballinger arrived, Ike took them to his mother, who wiped her hands on her apron and greeted them with respect.

195

Mother Ballinger said warmly, "We welcome thee to our meeting. It is good to be near thy children and thy grandchildren."

Now the children came rushing to the Ballingers. Cassie wondered if Mother Evans's frown was disapproval of the children's bounding spirits or envy of their love for their Ballinger grandparents.

Father Ballinger said jovially, "It is time we knew Ike's mother better. Thee must come into the living room and let these younger ones finish the meal while thee tells us about thy meeting in southern Indiana. We have heard some from Ike, but thee has earlier knowledge. What year did thee come and how? Did thee come on the Whitewater Canal?"

Father did have a way of putting people at ease. Soon Mother Evans had forgotten her determined sobriety. The children listened with surprise as she told of the long journey and how they had lived until Father Evans was able to build a comfortable house.

After dinner, Esther helped Cassie with the dishes while the two older women spoke of quilt patterns. Though Mother Ballinger was much younger than Ike's mother, she remembered the days of weaving and of the carding and spinning of wool.

Esther asked quietly, "Cassie, is it very hard for thee? Thy father and mother have softened Grandmother, but I do not think this is her nature."

Cassie smiled. "I have not my father's pleasant manner nor my mother's goodness. And Mother Evans does not find me plain or, I fear, a good wife and mother."

"Do not let her run over thee," Esther said fiercely. "Father should share this burden, and Uncle Wesley. She could visit me, but she would not. I could see she was ready to speak harshly to me when Ike and Thomas came in."

Cassie answered, "No doubt Ike will find a way out of our

problems. He is very wise, thee knows."

"Yes, and firm in what he feels is right. But thee had better be firm, too, or she will spoil thy home." Esther hesitated. "Already thy children seem less open, less happy."

"I try to be patient and kind, Esther, but she only finds me frivolous and worldly, like my father with his French name and blood."

Esther laughed. "Thee sees how he charms her in spite of her disapproval."

"I do not. I only make her feel it is her duty to change me."

"Don't let her. Not one bit. Grandmother will not help Thomas see the Light, that is sure!"

After Cassie had hung the dishcloths out in the freezing air, they joined the rest of the family before the big fireplace.

Too soon it was time for the guests to start home, but Cassie felt a warmth from the day that she was resolved to hold. Ike had helped them all by suggesting this dinner.

Cassie had suspected for several days that a surprise was in the air. Coming in unexpectedly from the garden, she had twice found Mother Evans flustered as she pulled her apron over some white material in her lap. The gathering with Cassie's parents and Thomas and Esther had gone so well and things now seemed so peaceful that Cassie was not surprised that Ike's mother should want to give her a gift.

Perhaps the surprise was a fine tatted kerchief for her birthday. Mother Evans's tatting had brought prizes at the fair.

Cassie's birthday came. At the noon meal, Ike's mother handed her the gift. Cassie held it with trembling fingers, thanking God for His help in lightening her burden. Surely this gift must indicate that she had gained grace in Mother Evans's eyes. Now her problem would be with Ike, to try to make him as he had been before his mother's coming.

Cassie removed the wrapping and gazed at the present, scarcely recognizing it, not crediting the idea that Ike's mother could so affront her. For a moment she held the gift in her hands, praying for strength that she might not rend it! At last she was able to say quietly, with only a tightness in her voice to show the anger she controlled, "Thank thee, Mother Evans."

With a quick motion, Cassie placed the carefully made cap on the braids of red hair, which Ike had once loved. She remembered his joy at seeing her in the green gown, with her braids hanging down over it. Well, let him deal with his mother. If this was the Cassie he wished to see, if approval from his mother was what he would have, so be it!

The children, also excited at a gift for their mother, had watched her open the package. They had looked in puzzlement as the cap was taken out, and now they stared at their mother under its whiteness.

Then Caroline's voice rose in a wail. "Take it off, Mother! Thee must take it off! It's ugly, ugly!"

Before Cassie could stop her, Caroline had struck at her grandmother. "I don't like thee! Thee is wicked!" she cried.

Cassie, in cold anger against this old lady, who seemed all that Caroline had said, turned to Ike. "Thee must discipline thy daughter, Ike."

Cassie watched him for the first time without the love and sympathy his distress had always held for her, watched his anxious face and bowed shoulders as he walked from the house without a word of blame to his daughter. Caroline sat crying in her small chair, gazing reproachfully at Cassie and the cap which covered her bright hair.

And Cassie knew that Caroline's grief was not for the thing she had done or the words she had said to her grandmother, but for the change that had come to her mother.

⤙XXV⤚

ALWAYS BEFORE, CASSIE'S BIRTHDAYS HAD BEEN JOYOUS. AT HOME when Cassie was a child, her parents had found them days for celebration, not only for her but for themselves. Then, married to Ike, they had been days of great happiness, days when she had felt even more cherished, though Ike was never able to give her fine gifts—only the gift of his love. The children had looked forward to her birthdays as well as their own.

But this was a new kind of birthday, a day that rankled in Cassie. A deep resentment grew as she washed the dinner dishes; she had abruptly refused to allow Mother Evans to help—more abruptly than she had ever spoken to her before. For Cassie knew that if she had to talk to her there over the dishes, words would be said that she might sometime regret. And if she allowed her to help and did not talk with her, it would be a kind of pouting and sullenness which Cassie did not like.

As Cassie worked, her mind darted round and round, trying to think how best to handle this problem, how to show Ike her great hurt—yes, her great anger. For she would not attempt to hide from him her affront at this gift.

Suddenly an idea came to her—not, certainly, a revelation of God's will, but a very human idea. Ike at least must see that he could not stand with his mother against her and find her love unchanged; it could not be that way.

All that afternoon Cassie worked to carry out her plan. The sewing machine was in the big kitchen, where they spent most of their time by the warm fire. Cassie sat at the machine and sewed busily at some white material, with no word as to what she made. Mother Evans watched, her old face questioning, but she would not ask, and Cassie carefully concealed the work

199

from her. This was between herself and Ike, but there was no privacy now in this house, and she could not take the time to make it by hand in her own room. When she was through, she folded it and carried it away.

That night, as Cassie prepared for bed, she stepped into the large closet and removed Mother Evans's cap from her head. Then she replaced it with another cap, tied under the chin with long strings.

Carefully she tucked her hair into the cap and stepped from the closet. She stood there quietly for a moment so that Ike could not miss the thing she wore, the fruit of her afternoon's labor, the companion to the gift his mother had given her.

As Cassie looked into Ike's eyes and saw his hurt, she turned away quickly so that he might not see the tears in her own eyes. She remembered his joy in her hair, his pleasure in holding the long braids in his hands. Sometimes in bed at night, he had stroked her hair and told her how beautiful it was and how beautiful she herself was.

But she hardened her heart. This time she must not allow her love for Ike to weaken her resolve to show him what was happening to their family.

Crawling into bed, she turned her back to him. No words were spoken. For what seemed hours, she lay there listening to his breathing until at last she knew that he slept—as though he did not care.

The next day, Cassie wore her birthday gift and sensed a feeling of triumph in the old lady's glance. Was the triumph because Mother Evans had struck a blow at vanity or a blow at Ike's wife?

Could it be right to hide beauty? Surely God did not want ugliness to flourish in the world. Was there not a kind of vanity in flaunting one's sacrifice of vanity? Indeed, vanity was wrong, but a proper respect for God-given beauty was not. And sometimes Cassie was persuaded that it was sinful to try to plaster down so firmly the curls God had given her.

So the days passed, a pain in Cassie's heart. Cassie was angry and hurt that Ike should allow such a state to exist, but also ashamed that she herself should foster such anger and resentment.

Three nights later, when Cassie stepped from the closet in her long, full gown and night cap, Ike pleaded, "Cassie, please take off thy cap."

"No, thee is ashamed of my red hair."

"Cassie, thee knows how I love thy hair."

"No, thee does not approve of love. Thee is ashamed of that, too."

When she lay beside him, her fingers were hungry to draw his head to her soft bosom.

"Cassie, why is thee so cruel to me?"

"I, cruel to thee, Ike? Thee knows I have only followed thy wishes. Even before thy mother came, thee knew that she thought me vain. Is thee like the miser who fingers his gold in his room alone? Does thee think thy children do not like to see their mother's hair? Must we all change to humor thy mother?"

Ike was silent. Cassie could feel him awake beside her, could feel his yearning for her love, for her arms to be around him. It was only by telling herself over and over of Ike's cruelty, his disloyalty in allowing his mother to change him and to try to change her and their children, that she could resist the wish to cry out her bitterness in his arms. But she would not, she could not.

Yet, if this was the right way, why did she feel this shame at what she did?

Everyone in what had seemed a happy family was becoming more and more unhappy. Only Ike's mother was her usual self, but with an added gleam of piety—or so it seemed to Cassie—

as her eye fell upon the cap that covered Cassie's red hair. No doubt, Cassie thought, Mother Evans felt she had come to a wicked and worldly household and reformed it, had rescued her son from evil, perhaps from his carnal nature. It was Mother Evans who now ruled Ike and Cassie's home, who treated Cassie as a child, a wayward child.

And Cassie had submitted, had contributed to her own humiliation in accepting the part of a child, and had blamed Ike.

She had betrayed all her parents' love and teaching! She had not been taught to handle her problems this way—with anger and cruelty.

For hours she lay in bed and thought of their situation, seeing ever more clearly that she had not taken the Friends' way to solve her problem. She had been so angered by Mother Evans's piety that she had lost the kind of piety Father and Mother had taught her; she had forgotten that the Light would come to her only if she made herself quiet, and allowed it to come.

Surely the Light would not come if she kept her heart full of anger, her mind full of resentful thoughts. It was wrong to hold anger in her heart; that she knew, had learned as a child.

Cassie had blamed Ike, and even now she could not think him blameless. Yet she knew his fault was not so great that she should withhold herself from him. She had thought his furtive lovemaking wrong, lustful. But by withholding herself until he did as she wished, had she not put a price on her love?

With sudden resolution, Cassie sat up in bed and removed her cap. She gently stroked Ike's cheek and kissed him. Quickly he was awake. "Cassie, Cassie, is thee ill?"

"No, Ike. Only ashamed of my treatment of thee."

As she leaned over Ike, her long hair fell around him. He sat up beside her and framed her small face in his hands. "Thy hair, Cassie; thee has taken off thy cap!"

Her arms were around him, and she murmured, "Ike, thee will forgive me?"

The barrier constructed by Mother Evans and by Cassie, the barrier Ike had not removed, was gone, and things were again as they had been before Ike's mother came.

The next morning, Cassie put on the cap Mother Evans had given her. She must not cause contention before some revelation came to her or to Ike about the answer to their problem.

They had talked long last night. Ike had said that he would not allow his mother to rule their home. They had prayed together for insight.

After breakfast, Cassie spoke to Mother Evans more pleasantly than she had during these long weeks. "I am going for a little walk. Will thee watch the children?"

Cassie walked through the early spring woods and sat down at last on a great log. She asked God to show her what she must do, to take from her heart the bitterness she had allowed to grow there. Then, in the greenness of the forest, she was quiet. Her mind no longer turned the problem over and over, but was content to listen and wait.

So quiet was she that the birds came out from their coverts and ignored her presence. As if from a far place, one called and another answered. Serene and waiting, Cassie felt a part of the quiet. No longer did she strive like Jacob for an answer to her prayers. She waited, her whole being open to God's will.

She did not know how long she sat there, had no care for her house or her duties, no worry for the morrow. "Take therefore no thought for the morrow; for the morrow shall take thought for the things of itself. Sufficient unto the day . . ."

The Light entered her spirit, and Cassie felt herself become one with God. Her heavy burden was lifted.

The words did not come to her as Ike's voice had come the

day of the well. It was as though they were there by no thought of her own. She now knew what she must do, what she must say when it came time for her to speak.

As she prepared supper that night, Cassie knew the time had come. This would be a day to remember, to mark the beginning of the return of love.

She would make this a festive occasion. She picked the spicy yellow roses from the yard and arranged them in her grandmother's lusterware pitcher. Their fragrance mingled with the odor of the warm gingerbread the children would enjoy. The snow-white cloth on the table was set with the thin silver spoons. They would have fresh bread and butter, cottage cheese with yellow cream, and wild strawberries the children had picked from the field nearby. The odor of frying ham, mingling with all the other smells of spring and of well-being, rose in Cassie's nostrils. Surely a likely time!

Cassie did not now feel concerned. If her heart beat a little faster than usual, it was not from fright or anger, only from the thought that this was a time of decision. God had shown her just what she must do and how she must do it.

At last, supper was ready and the table set. Cassie went into the bedroom and, standing in front of the mirror, took off the white cap, the birthday gift, and dropped it into a drawer—far back in a corner of the drawer.

She undid her hair from the braids and ran a comb through the springing curls. Then she pulled the front curls up loosely and tied a black ribbon around them, allowing the curls to fall over her slim shoulders, as she had seen in a picture in *Godey's Lady's Book*.

After washing at the pan outside the door, Ike entered the kitchen just as Cassie stepped in from the bedroom. He stopped short, and his loving and proud expression reminded Cassie of the way he had looked when he made his marriage vows.

Suddenly it was as if only the two of them were in the room, and they were again the people they had been before Ike's mother came. Though Mother Evans stood by the stove, she was forgotten as Cassie and Ike looked at each other, as feelings and thoughts stronger than any words passed between them.

Cassie could see Ike asking her to forgive him for not having taken a stand against his mother, could see that he was now able, if need be, to take the stand that must be taken. Then he turned and went to gather up the children for the meal.

Serenely Cassie helped the children into their chairs, smiling as Caroline put her fingers gently on her mother's hair and said, "Thee is so pretty, Mother." Even John chattered happily, but there was yet a little doubt in his face. How could he know, unless Cassie made him understand, that it was not righteousness that had made Mother Evans give Cassie the cap?

At last, finding her voice, Mother Evans said harshly, "Where is thy cap, Cassie?"

Cassie answered, not pertly, but mildly, "Thee may have it back if thee wishes. I shall not wear it again. I am not ashamed of the hair God has given me."

Mother Evans did not reply, and Cassie said nothing more.

Ike could not take his eyes from Cassie's face and seemed scarcely to know what he ate. The children were gay, and Mother Evans was quiet, a well-nigh threatening quiet.

When the meal was through, Mother Evans said, "I will do the dishes."

Cassie felt no need to insist that she herself do them. If it gave Mother Evans pleasure to feel herself put upon, it would give Cassie time with the children before they went to bed. She would read them the stories that Father Ballinger had brought them from the East. Lately she had neglected reading to them because Mother Evans always looked so disapproving. Cassie read until she felt they must go to bed. Though the children begged for "just one more," she tucked them in.

Coming back into the room where Mother Evans had now finished the dishes, Cassie pulled a stool near Ike's chair and sat leaning against his knees as he had liked for her to do before Mother Evans came.

For a moment, Cassie held her breath, half afraid that Ike would pull away. Then she felt his hard palm on her hair, felt the tension leave his body. She looked up at him and saw the tender smile she so needed and had so missed.

Mother Evans spoke, her voice shaking a little. "Since thee does not care for my gift to thee and wishes to make me feel unwelcome, it will be better for me to go to Samuel's to live."

Cassie felt a little tremor in Ike's knees and spoke quickly to spare him the answer she knew he would now give his mother. She no longer needed his support, since God had given this task to her. Quickly, but softly, she replied, "No, Mother Evans. Ike's mother will always be welcome here. But thee must become a part of the *spirit* of our family. If thee tries, thee, too, can learn to be happy."

She continued, with the softness now only a cushioning for the firmness in her tone. "But, if we make thee unhappy, not comfortable, the Lord has spoken to me, given me a plan for us. My parents gave us a sum of money when we were married, money which we have saved for a house we plan someday to build, one more to our needs and liking. We cannot build it all at once, but near our house we will now begin it. A little house for thee. Then, as we are able, we can add until it is the house we wish.

"Until that time, thee can be happier in a small house of thy own. Thee will not be bothered by our children or our gaiety, and if thee wishes to be sad, no curious eyes will watch. I am assured that this is the Lord's will. It was revealed to me."

Now Cassie turned her glance to Ike and saw the wondering gratitude in his eyes. She looked at Mother Evans's worn old face and felt no triumph at her defeat, only a great regret for the joy Ike's mother had never known—and a prayerful resolve that she herself might never again harbor the bitter resentment that had brought such unhappiness to their home, that had for so long closed her mind to the Light.

Then, with a bounding joy, she heard Ike's solemn voice say firmly, "The Lord's will be done."